a winter night

a novel

a winter night

a novel

by
anne leigh parrish

For information contact:

Unsolicited Press

Portland, Oregon

www.unsolicitedpress.com

orders@unsolicitedpress.com

619-354-8005

Cover Design: Kathryn Gerhardt

Editor: Analieze Cervantes; Caitlin James

ISBN: 978-1-950730-60-5

To John, Bob, Lauren, Lacey, and Sam

contents

"Winter is a season of recovery and preparation."
--*Paul Theroux*

chapter one

It's all about family, Angie tells the Greens. An elderly dementia patient can experience significant anxiety on their bad days. Love and support go a long way. The staff at Lindell is wonderful, in fact, they were given an award by the National Alzheimer's association just last year for their work in memory care. She assures them that their mother will get the best of everything. They're welcome to walk through the nursing wing, ask questions, and even chat with a couple of residents who still have a good grasp on things. Angie can tell them who fits that description—if they'd like.

Dan Green has the sour look of someone who is about to part with a lot of money—not his money, his mother's, but he's managing it for her. Angie assumes it's a sizable estate. Lorna Green and her husband, Joseph, owned a chain of grocery stores across the Southern Tier, the biggest of which was in Binghamton. Most people at Lindell are retired professors from Dunston University. Some, like Lorna Green, are business owners. It's a liberal community, solidly Democratic; yet, when asked how many other Jewish residents there are, Angie comes up short.

She returns to the idea of family engagement, and Dan Green says they won't have a lot of time for that. One daughter is heading off for college; another is getting married; the third is expecting a baby; and their son is pursuing his PhD in Physics at Princeton.

"Well, that's certainly a beautifully full plate, isn't it?" Angie asks, her voice light, and full of warmth and love for her fellow man. In fact, she thinks Dan Green's probably a jerk, not because of his curt manner, but because his wife looks all used up. Angie knows that look. She's seen it on the faces of her clients before she joined Lindell, when she wanted to use her Master's in Social Work to save women from the

11

abuse that comes from making bad choices about men. As Dan goes through the paperwork Angie gave him, Debbie Delaney comes to mind with her front teeth knocked out; her right eye swollen shut; a bruise the size of a baseball on her cheek; her two children sitting on the floor, playing with a headless doll and stuffed cat. Debbie went back to her husband when he got released, saying it was her fault; she'd made him mad; she didn't follow the rules. Angie can't quite see Dan as a wife-beater, but he's overbearing and probably selfish in bed.

This thought causes her to flush. She's sure they'll notice. Maybe they'll think she's having a hot flash. She's only 34 but might look older. If so, she doesn't mind. It's probably an advantage in her line of work. She made the mistake of mentioning this once to her mother, who was appalled. At 55, her mother could pass for ten years younger. Angie wishes she'd inherited her genes. Instead, she got her father's blond hair and gray eyes; her mother is a brunette. Nor are they built alike. Her mother is petite; Angie wears a size 16, and her therapist discourages her to dwell on this. It's hard on her self-esteem.

Dan Green wants to know how soon his mother can move in. Angie consults the spreadsheet on her computer. There's a vacancy now; the previous resident passed away just last week; the room just needs a fresh coat of paint.

Her cell phone buzzes on her desk.

"Excuse me just a moment," Angie says. She looks at the phone. There's a message from Matt. Why couldn't he have called her last night, when she was at loose ends and really wanted to hear his voice?

"What color?" Sophie Green asks.

"I'm sorry?" Angie says.

"For the room. The paint."

"Yes, of course. We offer a choice of seafoam green, sea breeze blue, pale daffodil, or pearl gray," Angie says and hands her four small paint cards bearing the hues she's just named.

"What's wrong with white?" Dan Green asks.

"Too antiseptic. She needs color. Color is very important. It nurtures the soul," Sophie says.

At this Dan turns a withering gaze on his wife, who meets his eye for just a moment, before looking down at the cards in her lap.

"I couldn't agree more. Color is crucial. Our paints are very carefully selected to be warm and inviting," Angie says.

Dan looks crossly at Angie, then returns to the forms he'll have to fill out for his mother to be admitted.

A few minutes later Angie's phone buzzes again, and again she takes a quick look. This time it's a text from her younger brother, Timothy.

"What does this mean, 'if a resident should decease before the end of any given month, no pro-rated fee for that month will be refunded on his or her behalf?'" Dan asks.

"Well, the rent is due on the first of the month—"

"With a five day grace period."

"Yes, that's correct. As I was saying, the rent is due on the first, and if your mother, or any resident, were to pass away any time during that month, you don't receive a pro-rated refund for the portion of the month the room is not occupied."

"What a racket."

"Mr. Green, I'm sure if you—" Angie stops when her phone buzzes a third time.

"Are we keeping you from something?" Dan asks.

Angie silences the phone and puts it in her desk drawer.

She says the no-refund policy is standard for retirement communities and nursing homes. They're welcome to explore other options. In fact, she encourages all families of prospective residents to do just that.

"Hm," Dan says.

"Miss Dugan didn't write the rules, Dan," Sophie says.

"Please, call me Angie."

She talks about the fitness center, the lecture series, weekly movies, and the art room, describing each in detail. She offers to take them on a tour so they can see for themselves.

"We already looked everything over. It's nice enough. That won't make any difference to Mom, though. She doesn't even know what day it is half the time," Dan says.

"She's bound to enjoy pet day. It's always a real favorite with the memory care patients," Angie says, then explains this is when a staff member brings in her own dog or cat to visit.

"Mom's allergic to cats."

"Well, please make sure you indicate that on the medical history form."

Dan continues to go through the pages, one by one. Minutes pass. Angie wonders why Matt's up so early. He doesn't start work until four. He tends bar downtown, a position that seems to agree with him on a number of levels—he can banter with the best of them, he likes being around people when they're drinking, and he digs the bands that come and play on the weekends. He was once an aspiring guitarist and will be again as soon as he can lay his hands on a good instrument.

Dan puts the papers he's been reviewing back in their folder. He looks at Angie.

"Mr. Green, I'm sure your mother will find this a wonderful place to start the next chapter in her life," she says.

"You make her sound like a book."

Angie laughs. She searches for something flattering to say and can't think of anything.

"I say yes," Sophie says.

14

"It's not up to you," Dan says.

"Your mother and I have been close for years. You know that. I think I know what she'd want if she were—"

"In her right mind?"

"Fully in possession of herself," Angie says.

Dan pulls out his checkbook with a heavy sigh. Angie explains that he needs to go to the Ombudsman's Office to sign the financial agreement and remit payment. He stands, checkbook still in hand, turns and leaves her office. Sophie gives Angie back the paint cards, then extends her hand. Angie shakes it. Her palm is clammy and nasty to touch. Angie has held many nasty hands in this business—sticky, bloody, callused, fever-hot, ice-cold, even one with three broken fingers. Sometimes the physical aspect of being a social worker is the worst of all.

Alone, Angie pulls out her phone and listens to Matt's message.

"Hey, it's my day off. You wanna get together for a drink? Call me."

Did he tell her before that he was off today? She can't remember.

Timothy's text says Matt was over at their place last night and made a crack about Sam's weight. Sam is Timothy's girlfriend. She's also friends with Angie. They met at Lindell before Sam quit to go back to school. Timothy and Matt have been friends for a while, which makes Matt insulting Sam all the more disturbing.

The second text is from Sam saying she knows Timothy already texted her about what Matt said, and that really, she's not upset about it.

Why didn't anyone get ahold of her yesterday—Sunday? And if Sam and Timothy invited Matt over, why didn't they have her, too? She thinks Matt probably went over to watch the game, Sam was probably on campus studying, came home, and they rolled into dinner without it being any kind of formal thing.

What the hell got into Matt, anyway? Angie carries a little too much weight herself. Does he think *she's* fat?

They've been seeing each other regularly for about a month and a half. They haven't slept together, though she wants to, very much, and he seems to want to as well, but they just can't manage it. They kiss great, they turn each other on, but then some chill seems to settle on them. As if they each secretly think that taking off their clothes and getting into bed is a very bad idea. For Angie's part, not liking her body makes it hard to let someone else touch it. She also assumes that when Matt imagines her undressed, he can't summon the necessary enthusiasm to lie naked against her.

But maybe she's read him wrong. Maybe he's as eager as she is.

She texts him back. *Sure, when and where?*

Her phone stays quiet.

She calls Timothy. He's on his way to work, at the Gap store in the mall. He says he just wanted to give her a heads up about what happened because she seems so into the guy. She asks him if he thinks she's making a mistake.

"Beats me. I mean, he's usually fine, but this was out of line."

"Are you guys still friends?"

"Yeah, but he needs to chill out and apologize."

They sign off.

She calls Sam who reiterates that it's no big deal. Matt was just in a weird mood. Angie wants to know what he said, exactly.

"That there's so much of me to love."

"Ouch."

"It's okay."

"You're a good woman."

"I don't know about that. I just don't care what Matt thinks."

Sam has a point. Matt is Angie's boyfriend, not Sam's. Timothy adores Sam, and that's what matters, right?

When they hang up, Angie registers that Matt still hasn't gotten back to her.

What if he's really just another flaky, insensitive idiot? It wouldn't be a surprise, would it, given the kind of man she always attracts?

No.

She refuses to give in to negative thinking. She's going to stay open, see where this thing with him might go, and push past the barriers between them—and within herself—to find happiness.

Assuming it even works that way.

chapter two

Sherry asks Angie what she thinks of her idea to engage some of the residents in an oral history project. Is she on board? Angie knows to say yes because Sherry's her boss and genuinely invested in the welfare of the Lindell community. Not that Angie isn't invested. It's just that she finds herself overwhelmed by her personal cynicism from time to time. It occurs to her that no one cares what any of these old folks have to say, then figures that's exactly Sherry's point. A voice, a story, some sense of agency regained.

Sherry was contacted by someone in the History Department at the University. The plan is to have students come in and conduct interviews. Did Angie know you could major in folklore?

She didn't. She has no idea what one would do with such a degree. Tell tall tales, no doubt. Hell, one doesn't need a degree for that. Just ask Matt. He never got back to her about that drink. She's called him four times in the last three days, with no response. She wants to go by the bar where he works but realizes that would look desperate. Sam and Timothy are quiet, too. Clearly, they've moved on from the awkward moment Matt caused.

"Who comes up with the questions?" Angie asks.

"The folklore students, I suppose. I haven't really thought about that."

Sherry is pushing 60. The pouches below her eyes speak to fatigue, a lifetime spent in the service of others, endless self-sacrifice. Sherry's devotion is compensated outside of work by the love she gets from her husband and five children, or so Angie believes. Sherry only mentions her family in passing. The husband came to the Christmas party the year before. He's a quiet, modest-seeming man who teaches

18

math at the University. Recalling how he looked adoringly at his wife as she sipped her glass of fruit punch makes Angie ache.

"You don't want them asking just the usual things, like where they were born, or what they did for a living because that's just collecting data," Angie says. "They need to say something like, 'Describe the hardest struggle of your life,' or, 'What's the one thing you're proudest of?'"

Angie's pleased with herself. Great ideas flow out of her when she least expects them.

Sherry leans back in her chair and taps her lower lip with a gnarled forefinger. Her polish is sky blue.

"That's good. That's very good," she says. She looks at her watch. She asks Angie if she'd like to take charge.

"Sure." Angie wishes she'd kept her mouth shut.

Sherry hands her a piece of paper with someone's name and an email address.

"Reach out to her, tell her we're really enthusiastic. We can't wait to get started."

Angie takes the paper and leaves the office. She's got a care meeting in a few minutes, and the thought of it makes her heart sink. Once a resident goes into the full-time nursing wing, these quarterly meetings become difficult. There are always tough health issues to discuss, and hard choices to make. Keeping one's distance and remaining objective isn't easy. On the night they met, at a party at Timothy's, Matt asked her why she chose a career where she had to deal with people who were messed up, one way or another.

"Because I'm good at handling messy people," she said.

After her second beer that night, she went on to talk about her father, Potter, who'd had a major drinking problem when she was young. It's why her mother eventually left him. At one point, Potter

19

had to move in with her because he got behind on his rent. Sometimes people can't help what happens to them, she told Matt.

"Yeah, but don't you get burned out?" he asked, sneaking a peek down the front of her blouse.

She does totally get burned out, but she's not going to think about that now.

Mr. Jenkins won't be attending his meeting today, though it's his right to. He made it clear he wanted to stay put. If Angie had to guess, he wasn't nice about it either. He's grown increasingly resistant to being bathed and dressed. He fights the toothbrush, the razor, and the comb, all wielded by patient, long-suffering hands. Though one aide, Carla, got a little rough with him the other day and was put on probation. She put him in a headlock, so she could get a washcloth to his face. Mr. Jenkins is usually quiet, but he howled "like hell," was how the floor nurse put it. That nurse, Ella, is present, as is Dr. Trane, and another aide, Susie. Mr. Jenkins' family lives out-of-state. Sometimes one of his daughters calls in and they put her on the speaker if she wants to ask questions. No one is calling in today.

The agenda is simple: How is he doing? Do we need to change anything? Ella mentions an increasing level of anxiety. Dr. Trane suggests Ambien. Susie says he seems to get the blues more than he used to. Everyone knows depression is not a normal condition, even for the elderly who get dumped, left behind, shut away, and ignored, but these are Angie's own words, not the accepted vocabulary.

Recently, her therapist noted a growing sarcasm about how she describes her work. Were she in a session now, she would be asked to consider if *she's* been dumped, left behind, shut away, and ignored. Yes, yes, no, yes. Well, she's shut *herself* away on occasion, becoming what her mother calls a hermit, her father a recluse, and her siblings a castaway. It occurs to her then, with shocking force, that if they all know this about her, why don't they do something about it?

Like what?

Like pulling me up and out.

Nancy, her therapist, often party to her internal dialogues, tells her that only she can do this for herself. The speed with which Angie closes this loop comes as a pleasant surprise. She is making progress. She is seeing herself more clearly than she used to.

Angie mentions the folklore project. She asks Susie if she thinks Mr. Jenkins might be interested in participating.

"He's not much for talking about himself, that's for sure, but I bet he could be encouraged," Susie says. She's in her early twenties and exudes friendliness and enthusiasm. Her zeal makes Angie feel old.

Angie confirms that Mr. Jenkins' end of life documents are in order. Not long after he arrived at Lindell, he signed a Do Not Resuscitate order against the wishes of his two daughters. The elder is listed as his Medical Proxy. She can make decisions on his behalf, should he become incapable, but cannot insist that life support be continued. Angie thinks, not for the first time, of the elderly people her parents will one day become. Her mother, widowed now for three years after her second husband got struck by lightning on a golf course, will go down fighting every inch of the way. Potter is more likely to benignly accept the inevitable, as long as there's a good glass of whiskey in it for him now and then. Despite his second wife's good influence and his own sporadic determination, Potter will leave this world loving liquor as much as he probably loved anything.

As the meeting concludes, Angie's phone buzzes inside the pocket of her jacket. Matt left a message! The icon on the screen is like a star hanging in the night sky.

But she won't listen to the message now. Let him be the one to wait this time.

She bangs out a quick email to Lynn Lowman, the University student organizing the interviews, suggesting they meet for coffee somewhere near campus. Angie likes getting out of Lindell when she can, even now, with winter socking in. Lynn answers right away that she's free tomorrow morning around ten. Would that be convenient?

Angie replies that it would. Should they try the Starbucks in College Town? When Lynn replies with a smiley face, Angie pauses before answering with *Lovely. See you then.*

This evening, she's having dinner with her father and his wife, Mary Beth. Mary Beth is a contractor. Angie doesn't care for her much. Mary Beth's manner is always courteously distant. Angie suspects that Mary Beth is uneasy with the close relationship Angie and Potter have. They never intentionally exclude her from their conversations, it's just that they have a way of reading each other's minds and finishing each other's sentences. The last time Angie ate with them, Mary Beth served up a bland orange soup she said was carrot with garlic. The woman might be out there building the most beautiful houses in and around Dunston, but in her own kitchen, she's a dud. Angie, on the other hand, is a pretty good cook, something Matt has remarked on several times, though all she's ever made him was a grilled cheese sandwich. It was the addition of goat cheese with a touch of honey that did it, she thinks. She suspects his tastes are pretty pedestrian in most things.

Her hand touches the phone in her pocket.

No, not yet.

She turns off her computer, puts on her coat, and shuts the overhead light in her office.

The sky is low and dark. The sharp smell of silver on the air says it will snow that night. She's not worried. It's a short drive from Potter's back to her place, and they're good about keeping the roads clear in the Heights, the section of Dunston they live in. Angie's mother lives there, too, in the house left to her by her late husband. She talks every couple of months of selling it and moving to Montana where she met someone on her weird cross-country trip right after her husband died. Timothy and Sam are about a mile away from her. Just down the block from Timothy's her youngest brother, Foster, is housesitting for a professor and his wife while they're on sabbatical in Paris. Angie's sisters, Maggie and Marta, live in New York City and come up at Christmas. That's the only time the siblings are ever all together. Angie thinks this is an artifact of the cramped quarters they endured for so many years in the meager rental homes their parents had them in. Only after her mother left her father and married a man with money did they have space to themselves. Or maybe their personalities just clash. She's seen enough family dynamics working at Lindell: a brother thinks his mother is losing her marbles, and a sister who says she's just fine, and neither listens to the doctor who says it's hard to know without further scrutiny. Or two sisters who can't agree on how much their mother should be asked to do to stay active. One says she should do what she wants to at her age, and the other thinks forcing herself to participate in an art class or mild exercise with the lady across the hall is the way to go. Families so often disagree. Maybe this is Nature's way of keeping everyone alert and on their toes; though, how conflict ensures the survival of the species escapes her.

At home, she is met, as always, by Peggy, her four-year-old tabby cat. Peggy glides across Angie's leg as she removes her coat. She wants to change before heading out again. The sober and serious pantsuits she wears to work are comfortable, but they don't do much for her. She recently bought herself a silk scarf in a lovely lavender tone that she pairs with several different turtleneck sweaters and blue jeans. The scarf improves her mood. She supposes that's why women like jewelry and perfume, too. Something to make them feel special.

Tiny snowflakes drift down as she drives to Potter and Mary Beth's. Their house sits behind a wide lawn. The stone lions on either side of the front door are a bit much. Mary Beth found them at a place that was going out of business and thought they were hilarious. Potter helped her wrestle them into her truck and threw his back out in the process.

Potter answers her knock and says Mary Beth isn't back from work yet. She called to say she was running late, dealing with a client who's flipping out about the cabinets he chose—ones Mary Beth advised against getting. Their evenings often begin like this, with a description of what's going on with Mary Beth. He concludes by saying the client is an idiot but always good for the payments.

"So, how are you?" he asks. They're in the kitchen, which of course Mary Beth remodeled after they moved in. The color palette is a soothing mix of blue, gray, and white with pops of red and green, like the scarlet tea kettle, and the lime ceramic bowl on the counter.

"I'm good. Tired, but good."

"Well, you look great. That's a really pretty scarf you have on, by the way."

Potter hands her a glass of white wine though she didn't ask for it. Angie doesn't drink much during the week, maybe a little more on the weekends, but she's always careful, aware of her consumption, because of him. He gets nothing for himself and says he'll wait for Mary Beth before diving in.

Angie remarks that something smells awfully good.

"Lasagna. Made it myself," Potter says, and suddenly Angie is cast back almost twenty years to the dismal house the family lived in right before their mother had had enough. Potter had cleaned up his act, temporarily at least, and made chili. He was out to prove he could be useful. It was short-lived. He soon went back on the bottle.

He asks how work is and she tells him about the folklore project. As she does, she wonders if someday the memory she just relived will be shared with a stranger as a way to keep her engaged with a world she'd rather just withdraw from.

"I want to ask you something. Did you know your grandparents?" Angie asks.

Potter scratches the back of his head.

24

"Well, I knew my dad's folks, but not my mom's."

"What were they like?"

"Tired and pissed off."

Angie laughs. Both of his parents were dairy farmers, and she assumes the grandparents were, too.

"Did they ever tell you stories about their lives?" she asks.

"Hell no. They were too busy making me mind my Ps and Qs. Your Aunt Patty's, too, though everyone always liked her a lot better than me. Boys get a bad rap. But I probably deserved it. I was a real stinker sometimes."

Angie sits on one of the padded counter stools and tastes her wine. She's heard many of her father's stories before. The first few attempts at sobriety caused him to ramblingly summon the past. Often, she was the only one around to listen. Still, she asks him now what he means, exactly.

"Well, I must have told you about the time this one crazy cow of ours kicked down the barn door," Potter says. This is a new story, and Angie says she would love to hear the rest.

The cow had just calved, and they put her in the small barn by herself to avoid the stress of being with the rest of the herd. Now, also on the farm in those days was a goose that wasn't quite right, by which he means it walked funny, sort of at an angle, flapping its wings as if it wanted to fly and couldn't. He can't remember where it came from. It seems to him as if it had always been there, wandering around, honking, getting in everyone's way. The cow and the goose developed a friendship, which wasn't as odd as it sounded. Farm animals did that. A pig could take to a puppy, or a lamb to a kitten, and so on.

After a day of being alone with her calf, the cow went nuts. She wanted out of that barn, and how! She paced, she lowed, she kicked the walls. They all took turns going down to try and quiet her. The goose could hear its friend's distress. It waddled up the little hill to the

25

barn and just stood there. The cow, maybe sensing its presence, quieted for a time. Everyone went on about their business. Then, after a while, the cow kicked the door down and bolted. They had a hell of a time catching her, but they did and put both her and the calf with the other cows. She accepted the calf, let it nurse, and was showing herself to be pretty maternal after all. Potter and his dad went up to the barn to deal with the fallen door. It was no easy task for the two of them to lift it, but they finally got it upright, and underneath it was one squashed goose.

"Oh, wow! I wonder if the cow knew what she'd done!" Angie says.

"I'm sure not. She was just glad to be out of there. Frankly, I always thought their relationship was pretty one-sided."

Potter has clearly enjoyed telling this tale. He pours himself a narrow finger of whiskey into a glass he's had at the ready.

"But how were you a stinker?" Angie asks.

Potter looks confused. It's not the first time he's gone off-topic.

"Well, just take my word, there were things I shouldn't have done," he says.

"Come on, like what?"

"Like taking my dad's truck out without his permission and running it into a ditch."

The cooler light in his eyes says the results of that mishap were unpleasant, probably spectacularly so. She asks nothing more.

When more time goes by and Mary Beth still doesn't come, they sit down and eat Potter's lasagna. Angie likes it, but it's dry. She doesn't say so. The one drink he's allowed himself makes him quiet and conversation hard. Angie lets it go. She's comfortable alone in her own thoughts for a little while.

"I hear your brother got a new cat," Potter says.

26

"Foster? Yeah, he told me."

Foster works in a vet's office and has his choice of the old and abandoned. This latest is a one-eyed destroyer he's named Mad Max. Mad Max has poor bladder control. Angie is pretty sure the nice rugs in the professor's house are already soaked. To clean them will be expensive, Foster will panic, call their mother, who will be reluctant, but then will give in and cover the cost for him.

They finish eating and go on sitting in the dining room where the lit candles on the sideboard flicker pleasantly. Potter refills her glass with red wine this time, then says he should have given it to her sooner since white isn't really what one eats with Italian food unless you've made chicken or fish. Potter isn't well acquainted with culinary niceties, and Angie thinks he's repeating something Mary Beth must have said.

Her phone trills its merry tune from her purse on the kitchen counter. After five rounds, it stops. Potter looks her in the eye to ask why she didn't answer it. She shrugs.

"Are you still seeing that guy?" he asks.

"Off and on. More off, than on."

"That's too bad. I liked him."

"You met him?"

"Yeah, at Timothy's pot-luck last month. You weren't there, were you?"

"No."

Angie had been on her way when she was called in to help handle an emergency at Lindell. A resident, living independently in one of their cottages, had attempted suicide. He left a note, saying seventy-five years on earth was enough for anyone, and now he was ready to go. He gulped down forty-three Ambien tablets and got into bed. It came to light when his daughter called and got no answer. The medics pumped his stomach. The first thing he said when he came to was,

"Shit." The staff had to go over his file, see if they'd missed something that would have alerted them to his state of mind, find a way to assure the family that he was in good hands. Angie didn't know Timothy had invited Potter, and Matt never talked about meeting him, which Angie now finds odd.

"He strikes me as your type," Potter says.

"How so?"

"Energetic. Ambitious. Good head on his shoulders."

Are they talking about the same guy? But Angie knows Potter tends to see people in a favorable light. It's part of his charm, and no doubt, without realizing it, he's drawn to that same charm in others.

Angie blushes when she realizes she's attracted to Matt *because* he's like Potter. Potter doesn't notice her high color, or if he does, he might assume it's from the wine.

The back door opens, and Mary Beth comes in, carrying a three-ring binder she slaps loudly on the counter. She leans into the dining room, takes in the fact that Potter and Angie have already eaten and sighs. Potter gets up, takes her coat, hangs it in the closet off the kitchen, and offers her a drink which she accepts. She's wearing a pink silk blouse and tailored black pants. She's reached the point in her career where the tools are held by others. She just supervises. Angie admires her professional success. Where her own career is concerned, there aren't many chances for advancement unless she wants to go back in the field again, which she doesn't.

Mary Beth takes the seat at the head of the table. She sips her scotch and tilts her head to one side, then to the other. Potter stands behind her and massages her shoulders. Mary Beth closes her eyes. She looks like a purring cat. Angie is uncomfortable witnessing such intimacy. After another minute, Potter stops and removes their dirty plates. He asks Mary Beth if she's ready for a bite and she says no, not just yet, thanks.

She talks about the Dillard remodel. Angie went to school with Lisa Dillard. Angie remembers her as unremarkable in every way. Now she's got a house that's getting a new kitchen, a new sunroom, and a new nursery. Angie's not sure why these facts are disturbing. Is it the nursery that bothers her? Does she want children? Is her biological clock ticking?

"It took her years to get pregnant," Mary Beth says. This seems like highly personal information for Lisa Dillard to share with her contractor. But she's heard details like these from Mary Beth about her clients before. Maybe she's a different person around them; softer, warmer, drawing out little confessions and making them feel at ease.

"Those fertility treatments are expensive," Mary Beth adds. She has no children of her own, and Angie can't tell if there is regret or envy in her voice.

Mary Beth and Potter talk a bit of shop and Angie's mind wanders. If she and Matt had children, what would they look like? Would they get her blonde hair or his brown? Gray eyes, like hers, or deep blue, like his? Would they be sturdy or sleek? What would they wake up and look forward to when they got to be the age she is now?

Mary Beth winds down. After a moment she says she had a call from Lavinia—Angie's mother—about remodeling her kitchen.

"Really?" Angie asks.

"Yup."

"Well, I think she might want to put the house on the market later this year," Angie says. Her mother complains about the house a lot. She lives there with her housekeeper and close friend, Alma. Lavinia says the house is too big, too cold, not modern enough.

"That must have been an awkward conversation," Potter says. Angie's parents are in regular contact and have been for years. She has no idea what they have to say to each other now, so many years divorced, with their children grown. It has occurred to her before that they still love each other very much, and this thought finds confirmation in the wary look Mary Beth gives Potter as his eyes fill with warmth.

"She was business-like. So was I," Mary Beth says.

"For sure," Potter says. He leaves and returns with a plate of food that he puts in front of her.

Angie reads their thoughts. He feels guilty for having affection for his ex-wife. Mary Beth wants to brain him for it and will keep silent until Angie leaves, at which point she'll speak her mind unsparingly.

Relationships are always fraught. Why are things between men and women always so hard?

Angie tells Potter it's getting late. She has a meeting in the morning at the University.

"Really?" Mary Beth asks. Angie recalls with an angry pang that Mary Beth once told Potter she didn't understand what Angie was doing in social work, but then also hinted that it was the only thing she could handle and do well. Angie still doesn't know why her father divulged that. Maybe he was warning her to stay on her toes in case Mary Beth said something mean. Ironically, it's only Angie's own mother that ever does that, but not for a while now, admittedly. And Angie isn't proud of the fact that her own tongue has sharpened over the years, especially toward her twin sisters, who have learned to avoid her most of the time.

"A student is working on a project that involves Lindell," Angie says. She can see Mary Beth isn't interested in the slightest, so she describes the situation in detail, embellishing an otherwise ordinary series of events with the lie that it was all her idea in the first place.

"So, that's why you were asking me about my grandparents," Potter says. His smile says he thinks she's clever.

"My grandparents were nuts, my mother's parents, that is. Never knew my father's. Anyway, my grandmother could talk your ear off, and my grandfather had nothing to say," Mary Beth says.

"I bet they both had interesting stories," Angie says.

"Probably not."

Angie rises, thanks them both, promises to be in touch again soon, and leaves.

At home, with Peggy on the couch beside her, she listens to Matt's message.

"Hey, sorry I didn't get back to you. Major weirdness going on at work. And I mean MAJOR, as in folks getting arrested. Let's hang out. I miss you!" He pauses. "Well, ttyl."

What was he going to say? That he loves her? Neither of them has yet said that. Angie because she needs to go slowly, and Matt no doubt because he doesn't feel it.

Yet, there was urgency in his tone. Of that she's sure.

She can hear Nancy telling her that there is analyzing, and then there is overanalyzing. This is definitely a case of the latter.

chapter three

Lynn Lowman is a surprise. There's nothing to suggest she's a student. If anything, she could be an artist. She's not young. Her tightly curled brown hair is streaked with gray, and Angie hopes when her own time comes, her blonde will better conceal time's passing.

The coffee shop they're in is just off-campus. It's noisy. The closely packed tables have caused more than one person to bump Angie's chair. Angie hasn't touched her decaf latté with non-fat milk. Lynn, on the other hand, is enjoying her hot chocolate with gusto. A thin brown line floats just above her upper lip. Angie avoids looking at it.

Lynn spent ten years working for the IRS, and she supposes that's where she got interested in oral history. She lifts one hand and says it's really not as strange as it sounds. People come in, explain their situation, why they can't pay, what challenges the year brought, and before long, they digress. At first, it used to really bother her. She had a schedule to keep, after all. She learned to gently interrupt and return to the matter at hand, which was always how to get Uncle Sam what he deserved. But one time she didn't interrupt for a few minutes, and really, in that business, sitting in a small, windowless office, across a desk from some guy running on about his problems, was quite a record.

The man that day was nothing special, nothing out of the ordinary, a carpenter if she recalled correctly, self-employed and struggling with the downturn in the housing market. The solution to his problem was simple: a structured payment plan that he could afford. He said he was sorry he'd fallen behind with the government and hoped business would pick up again soon because he loved to build. To make something was a gift, no, a calling really. His father was a master bricklayer, and his mother was a baker, so he supposed he had inherited good, capable genes. He didn't have children of his own, not yet anyway, and assumed when they arrived on earth, they'd be good with their hands, too.

Lynn tried to move him along and get him to say he understood what would be required from him every month, and what the penalties were for being late, but he was quiet only for a moment, appearing to listen politely, and then continued.

His grandfather built roads, and his grandmother made dresses for the women in her small Ohio town. He didn't understand people who didn't make things, who made money from shuffling papers around all day. He apologized if Lynn felt he were referring to her, which he surely wasn't, because it was clear that she, too, created something of value.

She asked him what that was.

"A way out," he said.

Other people had other stories, some told so she would feel sorry for them, lower their payments, overlook a few missed months, but for the most part, people spoke honestly about themselves and what they wanted from life.

Angie nods. She can't imagine anything more boring.

"So, I guess I became a good listener," Lynn says.

"It's an important skill, in any job," Angie says.

Lynn asks Angie how long she's been at Lindell.

"Six years."

"What got you into social work?"

"The usual reason, I guess. Wanting to help people."

"And why the elderly?"

Because she thought they'd be an easy population to interact with, unlike battered women, drug users, school drop-outs, released felons, and anyone trying to get back on their feet after a run of bad luck.

33

However, saying so might put her in a bad light. She casts about for a better response, and an incident she hasn't thought of for years comes back with a jolt.

"Well, I guess it's because of something that happened a long time ago," she says.

Lynn leans in closer. "What?"

Angie says that when she was 14, she and her family lived in one of the so many run-down rental houses that formed the backdrop of her childhood. Her father was out of work again. Her mother sold manufactured homes and had gone to a regional sales conference. Angie was in charge of her four younger siblings, and of her father too, which amounted to making sure he didn't drink too much.

One morning, she discovered that they were out of laundry soap, mayonnaise, and a bunch of other stuff. She wrote a list and deputized her brother Timothy, one year younger than she, to go to the store with the money she scrounged from her father's wallet and the spare change jar.

Here, she pauses.

Why hadn't her mother left them money for groceries while she was away? Her mother was—and still is—a highly organized person. She had never left the family on its own before, so maybe it just hadn't occurred to her. Angie thinks the real reason her mother forgot was that she was distracted by the fact that her boss had expressed a romantic interest in her. He was eighteen years older. Her mother clearly didn't have the same feelings for him, but she saw him as an opportunity.

Lynn looks at her closely, waiting.

"I told Timothy to take the other kids along, too, just to get them out of the house," Angie says.

"I would have done the same thing."

Anyway, off they went. The store was only a couple of blocks away, and Angie figured they'd be right back. They weren't. When they'd been gone an hour, Angie decided to go look for them. As she headed out the door, she saw them coming up the street. They had an old man with them. Her twin sisters, Maggie and Marta, were on either side of him, each holding a hand. He had on a pair of striped pajamas, a baby blue bathrobe, and black slippers. His eyes were empty. The kids explained that they found him sitting on a bench outside the store. They asked his name over and over, and where he lived. He just shook his head and drooled.

Obviously, he was senile and wandered away from whoever was taking care of him. Angie ordered everyone inside and put the old man on the couch. She sat with him.

"Wow, that must have been wild!" Lynn says.

"Not really. I just called the police, and they said his nursing home was looking for him."

Angie waited until the social workers came. Just before they did, the old man looked her in the eye and said "Caroline." Then he put his dry lips on hers and said, "Our love could light the world!"

Angie doesn't tell Lynn that part.

Lynn gets down to business. She wants to come out to Lindell as soon as Angie gives her a list of people to talk to. She promises not to take too long with any of them, maybe fifteen or twenty minutes per person.

Angie says it's probably a good idea if she's present at the interviews.

"Of course," Lynn says. She promises to send details by email that afternoon.

Angie's day at Lindell passes with the usual blend of frustration and boredom. After work, she finally returns Matt's call. She tells him to come over if he wants. He says he'd rather go out if that's okay.

He doesn't have to be at work until nine, so they settle on dinner at Angie's preferred Italian place. She arrives late, but only by a few minutes. A light snow falls pleasantly, making the warm dark interior of the restaurant welcoming and cozy.

Matt's at a table in the back. He's looking at his phone. The way his shoulders are hunched says he's tense. There's something uncertain in his face, a trace of worry perhaps. Does he think she won't come? As she closes the distance between the door and the table, she realizes again that Matt is ridiculously good-looking. All that thick black hair and eyes so blue they're lavender in some lights. She arranges a pleasant smile, one that says how glad she is to see him, but also suggests she still hasn't overlooked how long it took for him to call her back.

He stands, helps her remove her coat, and pulls out her chair. He's never done that before. She compliments him on his gallantry.

"My mother raised me right," he says. Is his tone defensive? The way he looks at her eagerly suggests not.

"I'm sorry I'm late," Angie says.

"It's okay."

"So, what's up?"

The waiter asks if they would like something to start with besides water. Matt asks for a martini. Angie, a glass of the house Chianti.

Matt says one of his co-workers got arrested for selling coke at the bar. It was in the paper, did Angie see? Angie shakes her head. Anyway, she'd been doing it awhile, apparently. The boss didn't know, or at least he told the police he'd had no idea, which makes sense since he's not there that much, but they didn't believe him, so he got arrested, too. His wife bailed him out. She's a mean lady already, and that probably turned her into a first-rate witch.

"How did all this keep you from being in touch?" Angie asks. She instantly regrets her words. Then she decides that if Matt is going to be in her life in a meaningful way, he has to get used to her directness.

"I had to take over. Double-shifts. I was beat when I got home. Just rolled into bed," he says.

Angie believes him. There's no reason not to.

She wonders if he'll tell her what he said about Sam.

Their drinks come.

He says he's missed her. It's been less than a week since they've seen each other.

"I missed you, too," she says. She touches his glass with hers.

She tells him about the folklore project, that at first, she thought it sounded silly, but is more interested in it now. The elderly are a great resource, something she always knew but hadn't really seen until she got talking to Lynn Lowman.

She's aware that he's not listening. His eyes are on the tablecloth, and he's nodding every time she pauses. She falls silent. He says nothing. Finally his eyes meet hers and she is overcome with dread. He wants out, it's clear. That's why he wanted to eat in public, where she can't cause a scene.

She drains her glass of wine. She flushes in an instant, glass still in hand.

"Look," he says. "I just have to ask. Why don't you want to go to bed with me?"

"Who says I don't?"

"Well, it's pretty obvious."

"Maybe I'm just shy."

He smiles.

"But, seriously," he says. "If that's not where you're at, that's cool."

Angie recalls their make-out sessions. Was she the only one who was afraid? Is Matt so confident in himself that it never occurred to

37

him that the whole episode could be a huge flop? Or do men not experience sexual flops, as long as the deed is accomplished?

"I don't want you to think I'm pressuring you," he says.

"What? No, that's not it."

"Then what?"

"I don't know. I guess I wasn't expecting this."

He takes her hand. His palm is solid. He brings her hand to his lips. The gesture nearly sends her off her chair. His advances have never affected her like this before. She reclaims her hand.

"Don't be nervous," he says.

"I'm not."

They order dinner and ask for another round of drinks, only Matt now wants wine, too. She asks about work, and if the mood in the place has changed, in light of what's going on.

Matt says everyone was scared business would fall off, but in a college town, that probably wouldn't happen.

"Who was it?" Angie asks.

"Who was dealing? Sharon."

Angie's only been in Matt's bar a couple of times but knows right away who that is from hearing people call her name in greeting. She's a short bouncy brunette who likes to give male customers backrubs as she puts down their drinks. A surge of hostility makes Angie's toes curl inside her boots. She's always hated flirty women. She's glad Sharon's in jail, though of course, she's probably out on bail now, too.

"Did she get fired?" Angie asks.

"Hell yeah."

Matt says one of the bands scheduled to play at the bar canceled because they didn't want to be associated with a place that sells drugs. Times have changed. You read what the Rock and Roll scene used to be like, and not that long ago, and it was drug city. Now? Everyone wants to be politically correct.

"They have a reputation to consider, like anyone else," Angie says.

Matt regards her slyly across the table. The alcohol has brought an attractive color to his face. His eyes shine.

"Is that it?" he asks.

"Is what it?"

"You're considering your reputation?"

So, they're back to this. He's gone from being someone who resists physical intimacy with her to someone who's having trouble keeping it in his pants.

Whatever distance he has traveled is all in her head. She has no way of knowing how he really feels about anything.

She eats her spaghetti. Matt practically inhales his cannelloni. He says it's the best thing he's ever tasted. Does she know how to make it? He bet she could do just as good a job.

"Sure," she says. "I'll make you a whole big batch."

He pushes away his empty plate and says, "You know what? How about if I call in sick tonight? They can handle the bar without me. Hell, after what I did for them, they should give me a raise."

"Well, I wasn't going to make it for you *now.*"

"That's not what I meant, and you know it."

His teasing smile does her in. It's too late to turn back. Tonight's the night.

chapter four

Nancy's office is a gem. It sits in the corner of a restored building downtown. One window faces north, the other east. The season's low light is mitigated by this arrangement. The building, once a department store, was built in the 1920s. Angie's mother took her to shop there when she was very young, before the owners sold to a developer who quickly converted the whole thing into office suites. Angie sits on a tan leather couch, a soft wool blanket in her lap, though the room isn't cold. If anything, it's too warm from the steam fed radiator in the corner. Nancy sits across from her in a deep chair, upholstered in purple velvet. Between them is a low coffee table, Danish in design, simple and sleek, and on the table is a box of tissues that Angie has helped herself to several times. She's been crying off and on for about twenty minutes.

Matt spent the night with her after their Italian dinner. They had sex. The sex was fantastic. Matt actually waited for her. No man has ever done that before, and it's thrown Angie into a panic. Nancy tries to delve deeper, but each question is met with tears.

Finally, Angie calms. She has no doubt what the problem is. In fact, it's very simple. Having now found something wonderful, she is convinced it will abandon her.

Nancy asks if she notices that she has said *it*, not *him*.

Angie knows she has a tendency to dehumanize or to objectify. She also knows it's a behavior learned from growing up poor with a stern, cold mother, and a warm, alcoholic father. Her fear of abandonment stems from her mother walking out, though she returned quickly enough to collect the children and drag them along. Angie has reckoned that interval of time again and again though it was only a matter of a few days. During that time, she didn't know what was going to happen, and the idea that the family would be rudderless was terrifying.

But would it have been rudderless? Wouldn't she, as the eldest child, have stepped up and taken charge? Is it the idea that she might have responsibility thrust upon her again that scares her? Specifically, that her issues with intimacy might have consequences?

"What if I do something to drive him away?" she asks.

"Like what?"

"I don't know."

Nancy reminds Angie that trusting others begins with trusting ourselves. If, in the future, there is a disagreement or point of stress, then Angie will have to be completely honest and open about what she feels and why—with herself and with him.

"Assuming I can figure it out."

Nancy's patient smile says that she will also be available to help her in that regard.

Since sleeping together, Matt has texted Angie every couple of hours. None of his messages are very deep or personal, things like *hiya, what's up, u still @ work?* She's answered some of them in an equally non-committal tone, *hiya back, not much, yeah, 'til 6.* She thinks he should say more, that they should both say more at this point, that relying on phones gives an artificial air and a sense of impermanence to everything. She doesn't share this with Nancy, because their time is up.

Once she's in the car, she calls Matt. It's early, only a little after nine in the morning, and she's pretty sure from the groggy sound of his voice that she woke him up. His schedule at the bar has him closing up at two a.m. She pretends to have forgotten this and is overly apologetic for the untimely hour.

"It's okay. I'm glad you called," he says. It sounds as if he's stirring, getting out of bed.

"Yeah, I figured we've been texting enough."

"Have I been doing it too much? You don't mind, do you?"

"No, it's fine."

"I just start thinking about you, and shoot one off."

"Me too."

That's not true. She hasn't initiated any of the exchanges. She just responds.

"When are we going to get together again?" he asks.

She pauses. She has to be at Lindell in an hour. Usually, she uses the time after her appointment with Nancy to go to the gym. The idea of sweating on an elliptical isn't appealing at all.

"Now, if that's okay," she says.

"Aren't you going to work?"

"Not until eleven."

"Cool."

She waits.

"Why don't I come over?" she asks.

"Really?"

"Don't you want me to?"

Now he waits. Is he hiding something? Is there something he needs to say and can't?

"Sure, I want you to. I need to shower," he says.

"I'm downtown. It'll take me about twenty minutes."

"Cool. See you soon."

Though Angie has never been to Matt's place, she knows how to get there, because he lives in an apartment complex Potter lived in right before he moved in with Mary Beth. She and Matt talked about that the night they met as they got the preliminaries out of the way. She's put him on the spot by inviting herself over. He won't have a lot of time to clean up. She assumes he's a slob because that's been her experience with all the men in her life. She'll be quietly surprised at the disarray; roll her eyes at the pile of dishes in the sink; delicately step over a discarded shirt on the floor; all the while conveying a patient attitude, one which suggests proper nurturing is what he needs.

Are you out of your mind?

She's not about to nurture Matt and show him the error of his ways. He's a big boy, and if he can't act like one, that's his problem.

Matt lives on the ground floor. This immediately strikes Angie as sad, though she also knows he would have taken whatever unit was available at the time. No one would *choose* to live on the ground floor, would they? Maybe he has a mobility problem, something that only crops up now and then, like a bad knee. How could that be? He's on his feet eight hours a day at work. And in bed, there's no problem there. She pulls into a parking spot marked "Visitor," turns off the car, and forces herself to breathe slowly and clear her mind. Too much doubt. Too many troublesome thoughts.

It's the place itself, she thinks as she goes along the cracked concrete path to the building. It reeks of the temporary, the rootless, somewhere people stay on their way to somewhere either better or worse. She's only channeling her own experience, though, of moving so often when she was growing up. Her family never seemed to stay anywhere longer than a year.

The smell of bacon frying greets her as she nears his door. Bacon is one of the many items she has taken off her list of regularly consumed foods, along with chocolate, doughnuts, pastries of any kind, ice cream, pancakes, waffles, and soda. She's sure she mentioned this to him. Does he have a bad memory?

But the bacon is being fried by the upstairs neighbor. Matt is in the middle of eating a bowl of Corn Flakes. His quick embrace sends a clean, soapy scent up her nose. His hair is wet, perfectly combed. His button-down shirt is pressed.

43

"Coffee's fresh if you want some," he says.

"Sounds great."

The kitchen is small and spotless. On the round table next to it sits a tiny jade plant in a terra cotta pot. The two placemats are made of tightly woven plastic. Angie has the same kind, though hers are red. Matt's are blue. She takes a seat. The mug he gives her has painted daisies on it. Her expression prompts him to explain that his mother bought it for him when he moved in.

"Where does she live?" Angie asks.

"Pennsylvania."

"Big state."

"Near Pittsburgh. Where I grew up."

Angie draws a blank.

"I told you that the night we met," he says.

"I remember."

She tastes the coffee. It's earthy, rich, with a mild chocolate overlay that's very pleasing. She relaxes.

He sits. His hands are on the table, palm down. His nails are trimmed and clean. The knuckles are bony and look strong. Has he ever had to punch someone out at work? But that's probably not what happens when someone acts up. They're just asked to leave. And if they refuse the police are called, right?

"Look," he says. "I need to make things up with Timothy. I said something I shouldn't have about Sam the other day."

"I know. He told me."

"I don't know what made me do it. Maybe I'd had one too many."

An unreliable drinker, eh? Given her own father, how familiar does *that* sound?

"Yeah, I think he wasn't too happy about it," she says.

"For sure."

Angie is glad Matt is sorry for insulting Sam, though she wishes she'd heard about it from him earlier. Maybe he was so eager to get her in the sack he didn't want to kill her enthusiasm.

She puts her hand over his. The sensation is electrifying. She hopes it is for him, too.

"I figure I need to smooth things over now, since you and I are, you know," he says.

She withdraws her hand.

"Are what?" she asks.

He struggles. Important words don't come easily for him, that's clear.

"Together," he says.

What the hell were they before?

She nods.

"I mean, we're bound to see them, right? Can't have a thing like that hanging over us," he says.

"Over you, you mean."

A sharp light flashes in his eyes. "Yeah."

"I think it's a good idea. I know he'll appreciate it."

"He's a good guy."

"I think so, but I'm biased."

"A sister *should* think well of her brother."

It's an odd remark. Angie casts her mind back. Did he mention a sister? She remembers him talking a little about the mother.

"Yours doesn't think well of you?" she asks. He says nothing. He takes her empty mug to the sink, rinses it out carefully, and puts in in the stainless-steel dish drainer. Then he washes his breakfast bowl and spoon.

45

He turns around. "Here's the deal…" he says.

Sis has a drug problem. She's been running around with meth monkeys since she was 17. The current boyfriend is in and out of jail. He's months behind on child support payments to the mother of his two children. Plus, he has anger management issues. He gets ticked off super easily, and before you know it, flattens some dude in a bar for looking at him sideways. Matt gave her money for a while, then just couldn't anymore. Saying so earned him a bitter, childish tirade with some very colorful insults. That was almost a year ago. His mother won't deal with her either. It's been hell because he worries about her, but he can't deal with her drama.

"She needs help," Angie says.

"We tried."

"Professional help, as in counseling, rehab, changing her peer group."

"You're preaching to the choir."

He faces the sink again and wipes down the sink with a sponge. His sorrow is clear in the slope of his magnificent shoulders.

Angie considers his earlier remark about them. She's not sure how she feels. She's crazy about him, that's true, but maybe she's *too* crazy about him. Maybe she needs to really think this whole thing through. She doesn't want to move too fast.

What's wrong with you?

She stands, approaches, and wraps her arms around him from behind. She presses one side of her face to his shoulder blade. He turns off the water, turns, holds her hard, and kisses the hell out of her.

"Thank you for understanding," he says, still holding her.

"I'm an understanding person."

"One of the many things I love about you."

She releases him and turns away.

46

Love?

She picks up her purse, looks at her watch, and says she'll be late if she doesn't get going.

"Come by the bar later. Tuesdays are always slow," he says.

"Won't be until around eight. This is my late day at work, and I need to grab dinner."

"I'll comp you a burger."

"I'll still need to go home and change, first."

"You look fine."

She's wearing another one of her dull navy-blue pantsuits, which she's dressed up just a little with a costume jewelry brooch on the lapel. It was a poor choice, she thinks now. It makes her look like she's trying too hard.

"You need glasses," she says.

He smiles. "Nothing wrong with these eyes. Not when I'm looking at you anyway."

They kiss again, not as long this time, and she's on her way.

chapter five

Vivian West is the first to be interviewed. Though she accepted the invitation to talk about herself, she's not happy to have people in her room. She's not happy about being out of bed, either. Her wheelchair is positioned so that the thin daylight falls on her hands, folded in her lap. Angie can't stop looking at her hands. She's seen hundreds of old hands, but Vivian's are well-cared for. Someone has applied pink nail polish, her granddaughter perhaps, who tries to come by every other week. Vivian's son lives in town too, but he never comes around. After a few minutes, the incongruity between the smooth nails and the thick, gnarled veins becomes hard to look at, and Angie finds another focal point, a small framed piece of needlework on the wall behind Vivian. It's a prim little cross-stitch of a house under a blooming tree, the kind of thing you could pick up at an antique store for about two dollars. The idea of Vivian's much younger hands wielding needle and thread depresses her.

Lynn Lowman sits in a folding chair directly across from Vivian. Angie is in another chair next to Lynn. Lynn uses her cell phone as a recorder and asks Vivian to state her name. Vivian's voice is surprisingly strong.

Angie curls her toes tightly in her tan pumps. Why is she so tense? Vivian is just an old lady, a bit put out, who's looking at Lynn as if she were a door-to-door saleswoman.

Lynn asks her to take her time, really think, then share something from her long, wonderful life. One of Vivian's white eyebrows lifts. She shifts in her chair, pulls the crocheted blanket up a bit, tugs at the sleeve of her yellow sweater, the cuffs of which are decorated with roses.

"Wonderful? Yes, much of it quite wonderful. Less so now, of course. Woe unto thee, seen to by strangers. Caring strangers, I will admit." Vivian nods at Angie.

Angie has had very little interaction with Vivian. Vivian is basically on cruise control. Her condition is steady, she comes to her care meetings, looks through her folder herself, corrects the nurse when she errs about what medications she's on, which doesn't happen often, thank god. She's an easy resident. Angie can't remember the last time they talked. The Christmas party last year?

"I was born in England in 1932. The height of the Depression. Or, should I say the depth. Dad was out of work. He was a railroad man. Managed the switches. Swung the lanterns. But when service was cut back they didn't need him anymore. We came to Boston, first. Things were as bad there as they were in Leeds. My mother had a talent for sewing, and that's how she found work. Anything that used a needle and thread, she was your girl. Curtains too long? No problem. Wedding dress too tight? She knew about that, too. Rumor is I was born only seven months after they married. But that's human nature. Who am I to judge?"

An aide comes in to ask if Vivian needs anything. The aide is a recent hire, Lisa something. Her hair is done up in a tight French braid. Her smock and slacks are brilliantly white and perfectly ironed. This is a girl who gets up early and throws herself into everything, Angie thinks. She bets she's a good bowler, too. Vivian waves her off, then summons her back. She takes Lisa's hand and tells her she appreciates her. She drops the hand, points at her and says, "Don't *ever* let anyone *not* appreciate you." Lisa smiles indulgently and leaves.

Vivian continues. She jumps ahead decades to her marriage and her only child, a boy named Roger.

"Named after my father. We fought about that, Edgar and I. He didn't think I had the right to choose his name. Who had a better right? I gave birth to him, after all. I carried him under my heart for nine long

49

months, sick most of the time, still teaching mind you, then coming home to cook Edgar's dinner. That man was awfully fond of my pork chops. Ate them the day he died, though I hesitate to find a connection there."

Vivian laughs a throaty laugh, followed by a brief fit of coughing. Lynn hands her a paper cup containing water she has strategically placed on the side table holding her cell phone. Vivian declines the water. She pats her hair. Her eyes wander the room. Angie can see that she's gone off track, lost in some other time and place.

Then she focuses.

"Roger and I had a falling out. A rupture. Our relationship split down the middle and never came back together. I haven't heard from him for . . . oh, I don't know. Twenty-two years? I have friends who tell me to rewrite my will, not that I have all that much, but whatever it is, he gets. Why shouldn't he have it? It's not his fault that he can't love or even respect me. I'm not saying it's *my* fault, please don't misunderstand. It's just a sad thing that happens between people sometimes, though believe me, I didn't see it that way for a very, very long time."

There were bitter fights, she says, recriminations, insults made on both sides. She didn't accept his accusations; then later, he wouldn't accept her apologies. Perhaps if she'd had a daughter or another son, someone to lessen the intensity of their relationship things would have turned out better. D.H. Lawrence certainly knew what he was talking about, didn't he?

"I'm sorry?" Lynn says.

"*Sons and Lovers*. Published in 1913."

"I thought Asian history was your field."

"Yes. But I'm also well-read. No one can claim to know anything of value if one doesn't acquaint oneself with great novels."

Angie needs to get back to her office now, she has a new family to interview, several files to go over, and a meeting with Sarah, the director of activities, about the coming holidays. They will debate encouraging the more introverted residents to participate in a sing-along. Last year it wasn't too popular. Only three people showed up. Then there's the matter of afternoon tea—a daily event that is enhanced once a week by offering a movie. Some residents love the old black-and-whites. Others want something newer, something their grandkids would like. Angie doesn't see why they can't just alternate, but Sarah wants to be totally fair to everyone.

Only you can't be totally fair to everyone. Fairness, like love, has a limit. There's only so much to go around. Vivian's son would know just what she's talking about, wouldn't he?

Lynn tells her she'll be in touch about the next interview.

The day goes by. Snow falls, then stops as Angie gets in her car. Despite Matt's admiration of her outfit, she goes home to change and to feed Peggy, who is found roosting on top of the refrigerator.

Matt texts that he is looking forward to seeing her. She replies with *Me too*.

She wears a black wool dress and a pair of heavy tights. She pulls on thick socks and slips on the cowboy boots she got in college. The boots were used when she got them. They're scuffed and extremely comfortable. She examines her reflection in the mirror over her bedroom dresser. The dress slims her. She should wear black more. Black makes a statement the way that brown and navy blue never can. She wishes she had a heavy silver necklace to put on, something long and ornate, maybe a Native American design full of sky-blue turquoise. Angie wants to visit the Southwest. One of the Lindell residents has stunning sepia-tinted photographs of saguaro and stone spires on the walls of her room.

The temperature has dropped. Her breath is a silver plume. The sky is thrown with stars. She wants to turn around, go back inside, light a fire, sit under a blanket with Peggy in her lap. She backs carefully out of the garage, remembering the one time she cut too close and scraped her car. Life is full of mistakes, things to avoid repeating, paths not to go down.

That's an awfully dark view, though. She needs to lighten up.

Matt's bar is called The Watering Hole, and the interior is as hackneyed as the name. The black-and-white floor tiles are dingy; the red vinyl booths are cracked; the tin ceiling is pockmarked; there's a wooden platform at the back that's used as a stage. The crowd is for the most part young. A woman sits on a stool, with a guy on either side, both of whom are talking to her, trying to lay claim. She plays it cool, not looking at either one, just sipping her frothy drink, and twirling her long hair now and then with her free hand. The booths are full of couples except for one, where a middle-aged man sits with a sandwich and a newspaper. Angie recognizes him from somewhere.

Matt is behind the bar, looking very dashing in his button-down shirt with the sleeves rolled up to the elbow. The woman on the stool turns her head as he draws near to ask if they need another round. Angie approaches, and when Matt sees her, he comes out from the bar with a winning smile. He takes her coat.

"You look great!" he says.

"You too."

The woman at the bar watches them in the mirror. Angie kisses Matt on the mouth. He steps back quickly.

"Hey, working, remember?" he says.

But he's not put out by her affection. His eyes say he can't wait until his shift is over.

He shows her to a booth near the back. His break is coming up, and he can hang out with her while she eats. She tells him to ask the cook to make her burger medium.

"But hold the lettuce and onions," she adds.

"How about a beer? Got a new IPA on tap."

"Sounds great."

He salutes and strides into the kitchen to deliver her request. Then he returns to the bar and mixes up three more of whatever the woman and her escorts are enjoying this evening.

Angie waits for her beer and lets the day slide away. She thinks ahead to the holidays and how much she will be able to see of Matt then. She and her siblings have dinner on Christmas Eve with their mother and Alma, where the tone is generally quiet, sometimes tense. On Christmas Day the party moves over to Potter and Mary Beth's where the mood is lighter. Potter is responsible for ninety percent of the cheer; Mary Beth grudgingly contributes the rest in the form of good food—provided by a specialty gourmet store—and excellent wine. She knows a vintner in California, and he cuts her a deal. By the time dinner's over, Angie's a wreck from so much time in the company of her kin. The mood at Lindell is equally difficult, full of false cheer and enthusiasm, though to be fair, some of the residents seem to have a great time.

Another server drops off the beer. Matt's got his hands full with a new group that's occupying four stools. The woman with the two guys is getting ready to leave. It looks like the guys are trying to decide who's picking up the tab. Angie wonders how the evening is going to end. Will she go home with one of them? Neither of them? Will they all stumble into bed together? On their way out, she looks at them closely. The woman and one of the men share a likeness—round face, long nose, pointed chin. Ah, of course, a sister, her brother, and the brother's friend who hopes to become the sister's boyfriend.

Matt catches her eye. He's shaking something in a silver container, probably a martini. He pretends it's hard work, takes a break, and wipes his brow. Angie rolls her eyes and smiles. She tastes her beer and enjoys the rich, bitter overlay. She drinks down a third of the mug, leans back and feels a warm mellow wave wash over her.

Why can't she feel like this all the time? She should become a Buddhist. Calm, centered, at peace with the universe. There's a temple downtown, not far from this bar, in fact. She's seen the monks walking along the sidewalk, their shaved heads gleaming; their robes billowing in the breeze, making them seem full of sublime spirit. To spend your life seeking total serenity sounds ideal. You'd have to put some serious distance between yourself and the world to do that. You'd pretty much have to turn your back on it.

She sits, sipping, and calls to mind the black-and-white photograph that hangs across the hall from her office at Lindell. In it, a stream flows over small rounded rocks. The rocks are dark, the water light, sparkling in places. The rocks have been smoothed over time, worn gently, almost lovingly by a steady flow of water that has no beginning, no end. In her sessions, Nancy sometimes asks her to pick something calming to think about when she's stressed. Angie has never been able to come up with anything that works. She's tried fluffy clouds, a clear pane of glass, even a blue stone she found once as a child on the beach of Lake Dunston among thousands of gray ones. However, this image now of the stones and water is very soothing and transports her to the shores of the stream, where she sits on the soft grass in a comfortable dress that fits her perfectly. She becomes unaware of her physical self, and all she dislikes about it. She is connected to the ground, sky, and everything around her. She is free. She is—

A tray of beer mugs crashes to the floor. Chairs are pushed back, people are on their feet, Matt rushes out from behind the bar with a broom and dustpan. The server who dropped the tray stands miserably over the piles of shards, looking like she's about to cry. Matt says something to her, puts his hand on her shoulder, then briefly rubs her back. Angie tenses. He goes awfully far with his consoling, she thinks, then tells herself to chill out, that he's just trying to be nice.

The mess is removed, everyone is back in their seats, the atmosphere settles. Music comes up on the jukebox, a song from the seventies, a southern rock band Angie knows and can't remember the name of. It's got a great beat, fast, gorgeous harmonies, but her lovely mood is gone now, replaced by realizing she's pretty hungry. Where the hell is that burger?

The man she thought she recognized on her way in stands by her table and asks if she works at the Lindell Retirement Home.

"I do, yes," Angie says.

He extends his hand. She clasps then releases it.

"I'm Harry Mason. I met you when my mother was dying. Last year. Jane Mason?"

Angie recalls a tall, gaunt woman, with a fierce, predatory gaze as she sat silently in her wheelchair in the dining room and refused to eat. She was the widow of a retired professor; astrogeophysics, Angie concluded from the star chart on the wall of their shared bedroom in the independent cottage they rented where he died in his sleep. The wife's horror at discovering him unhinged her enough to land her in full-time nursing, though as far as the psychologists and doctors could tell, there was nothing wrong with her mind. Angie remembers wondering what it would be like to wake up next to a man you've slept with for fifty years and see that he wasn't breathing and icy cold to the touch.

She invites Harry to sit. He asks if she's sure he isn't bothering her.

"No, no, not at all. I just ordered something to eat. Won't you have something, too?"

"Oh, I already ate. I was on my way out when I saw you here."

He's brought his drink with him. It looks like scotch or bourbon on the rocks, her father's favorite, except when he skips the ice and just sips it straight.

Matt delivers her burger. Angie introduces him to Harry. Harry doesn't offer his hand; neither does Matt. Angie eats; Matt stands a moment longer at the table, then leaves. Harry stays put. He works on his drink while Angie plows through the burger. It's pretty good, but there's too much mayo on the bun. She'll have to remember to mention that to Matt.

"How are you getting along since you lost your mother?" Angie asks.

"Okay, I guess."

"You were close."

"Not really, but she was always *there*, you know?"

"Yes."

She's heard this from family members before. Missing someone is hard and difficult to adjust to, but the alteration of one's personal landscape also jolts. When one has always had a mother, what is it like to be suddenly motherless?

Harry says his sister took it better than he did. She's over in Albany, though Angie probably knew that.

This, too, is familiar, the assumption that passing encounters mean Angie is fully acquainted with facts she can't possibly know.

He says he's pretty sure his wife is doing just fine. They didn't get along, his wife and his mother. He supposes that's fairly common, right?

"I couldn't say," Angie says. She's tired of Harry now and wishes he'd finish his drink and go home.

Matt takes her plate off the table and stares at Harry.

"Nothing more for me," Harry says and puts a twenty-dollar bill on the table.

"Change?" Matt asks.

"You keep it. You run a nice place here."

"Not my place, but thanks." Matt leaves.

Harry works himself up and out of the booth. He runs his hand over the back of his hair.

"She was a nice lady, my mom," he says.

"I'm sure she was."

"Never had it easy. Not a single day."

Angie nods.

"My wife doesn't know anything about that. I take good care of her."

"You give her my best," Angie says. She knows for certain she never met this wife. Only Harry came to Lindell to collect his mother's belongings.

After Harry goes on his way, Angie tries to restore her earlier mood and can't. She looks around for Matt. He's behind the bar, sees her, and comes over.

"Lonely?" he asks.

"What?"

"Since your boyfriend went home."

"What are you talking about?"

"I was going to take my break and hang out with you while you ate, remember? So, I look over here, and you've got plenty of company."

Angie points to the empty seat, and Matt slides in across from her. She explains who Harry is and how she knows him. Was she just supposed to turn him away? She didn't seek him out, Matt must have seen that from where he was. What's the big deal, anyway?

Angie's voice is harsher than she'd like it to be. Matt leans back, a hurt look in his eyes.

"I wanted to spend some time with you," he says.

"Well, here I am."

"Yeah, but my break's over."

"Already? In that case, how long would we have had, anyway?"

She feels herself rolling towards an edge she doesn't want to reach. She's being mean and can't help it. She needs to see it from his side, apologize, suggest another time away from the bar when they can hang out, reassure him that all is well.

But she can't.

"I have to be nice to people. That's my job," she says.

"So be nice to me."

She breathes. She takes his hand and grips it hard enough for it to hurt. He doesn't seem to mind.

She tells him to come over when he's off shift. Maybe zip home and get a change of clothes for the morning?

He says he should probably stay over at his place. Timothy's coming by first thing for coffee. He suggests that she spend the night. The idea of seeing Timothy right after rising from Matt's bed doesn't sit well. She knows she tends to compartmentalize things, and that this is a chance to work herself out of that behavior, but just can't face it.

"Let's make it another time," she says.

"Okay."

He sounds fine, no trace of disappointment.

"I'm sorry about Harry," she says.

"It's okay. I get it."

Again, he sounds fine, no trace of his former irritation.

He walks her out, touches her shoulder, and goes back to work, just like that.

At home, she asks Peggy if it's normal for someone to get over things so fast. Does it mean he's shallow? Not really there? Peggy stretches her furry legs and purrs. She's used to being interrogated like this and quickly goes back to sleep.

chapter six

On Saturday evening, Sam drops by Angie's place. Angie makes a pot of tea. Sam's very into tea and frequents a new specialty tea shop on the Commons—the downtown pedestrian mall. She brought over a fresh tin of Chai Matcha. She says it's energizing. Before Sam's enthusiasm, Angie wasn't much of a tea drinker. She thinks her lack of interest comes from urging so many Lindell residents to take part in the daily tea service. She's attended many of those herself, even pouring out cup after cup of thin brown liquid into plain white cups. Out of respect for Sam's passion, Angie recently bought a porcelain teapot decorated with painted green lines, flowers, birds, and bees. She has a set of matching cups and saucers. When she sets everything out on the coffee table in her living room, the effect is calming.

Sam's wearing a pair of black corduroy coveralls and with a green turtleneck underneath. Angie wonders if a beret sometimes completes the outfit when she's really feeling the poetry muse. At least one of her professors thinks she's got talent. Angie wishes that didn't make her feel jealous. She tried her hand at poetry once and she sucked at it.

Sam tells her about Matt's apology. Timothy went by Matt's for coffee and Matt said he was sorry as hell for suggesting Sam wasn't wonderful.

"He said that? 'Wonderful?'" Angie asks.

"Yup."

"Wow."

Matt also said he'd been in a rotten mood that day, which was why he drank too much. He'd run into an old girlfriend at the store. Right out of the blue. He didn't think she even lived in Dunston anymore, at least he thought he'd heard she'd moved away after they broke up. She'd put on a lot of weight. He said nothing to her about it, of course. He figured he must have had excess weight on the brain when he made the dig at Sam.

"Ex-girlfriend," Angie said.

"Yeah."

"He never mentioned an ex-girlfriend."

"Well, it's still early days, right?"

Angie stares into her tea.

"Did you mention any of your exes?" Sam asks.

"No."

"Well, there you go."

There are only three.

Blake Rawls was her professor. He had a reputation of getting cozy with his female students, though not all liaisons led to the bedroom. The time Angie spent in his causes a fearsome pang. He was her first, a fact she admitted as coyly as she could, the delicacy of the situation destroyed by his shrug. The whole exchange felt mechanical; she could have been anyone. Once she had served her purpose, he was on his feet and in the shower, singing no less. She broke down. He told her to get a grip, then to grow up. This is how things were between men and women. The sooner she understood that, the better. She had no one to confide in, no one with whom to compare notes. She kept her misery to herself as best she could until she had to confess the whole thing to her prying, watchful mother.

After Blake came Brett, a graduate student in Economics. She didn't feel for him what she felt for Blake, and at the time took that as a good thing. She'd gone up the romantic learning curve. She could hold her own and not get swept away. She was betrayed again soon enough, not only because he didn't return her affection, but because he took blatant advantage of her. They were living together in a home her stepfather bought, the one she still lives in. She paid the rent, though it wasn't required. Standing on her own two feet was important. Brett contributed nothing, pleading a student's poverty, though Angie knew for a fact that his family back in Minnesota was well-off. The end came when he said he was visiting them for a week, but instead was staying with another woman nearby. Angie cried, put his belongings in a couple of garbage bags on the front porch, and changed the locks.

The last connection was with a newly-divorced man whose father was a Lindell resident. Angie felt sorry for him. It helped that he was good-looking. That was one thing all her men seemed to have in common. Jerry was ten years older than she was, but looked upon her as a mother figure, something underscored by learning his mother died the year before. She decided he was a sensitive soul and warmed to him. He reciprocated, which meant talking for hours about his ex-wife and how she had failed him. Once, Angie said it was hard getting into bed with a ghost between them and he sulked for days. Neither of them broke it off. They just sort of fizzled out.

"Did you tell Timothy about your exes?" Angie asks.

"There aren't any."

"Seriously?"

"Yup."

So, Timothy is the love of Sam's life.

"And it's all good between him and Matt now?" Angie asks.

"Seems like it. They're talking about getting tickets to see the Knicks sometime next spring."

"Matt likes basketball?"

"Apparently."

Sam asks how work is. Angie says it's the same. Also that she doesn't like it as much as she once did. She thinks she might want to make a change, start a new career, maybe go back to school.

"Cool," Sam says. She sips her tea. "What other careers can you see yourself in?"

"Teaching?"

"Interesting."

"I figure old people are a lot like children, so I'm already most of the way there."

Sam laughs.

"What subject?" she asks.

"What subject what?"

"Would you teach?"

"I don't know. Reading, writing. Something easy."

Sam's eyebrows lift. She says there's nothing easy about writing. And as far as she knows, getting a child to be a successful reader can be really tough. Some of the graduate students who teach large lectures in her department serve as mentors in the local schools. They say it can be hard to keep a kid engaged. There are all kinds of techniques to make learning fun. It's almost a whole field, in itself.

"For sure," Angie says.

Sam puts her cup in her saucer. Her hands rest easily in her lap. She regards them for a moment. They're big, and strong, like the rest of her. Angie knows Sam had body image problems when she was younger. They talked about it after they first became friends. She seems very comfortable with herself now. Angie is sure that Timothy's wholehearted love for her has helped immensely. To receive unconditional love is a gift. To be able to accept it is another, rarer gift.

"You're about as interested in a teaching career as you are in selling cars for a living," Sam says.

Angie laughs loudly. "It did just occur to me, that's true."

"You're such a phony."

"But I *am* thinking of quitting Lindell."

"Fair enough. It gets old. No pun intended."

They're both laughing now. Sam says that if she's got any money saved up, she could coast for a while until something catches her eye. Angie has about a year's salary put away. She's frugal, the house is now hers, and her mother is generous, though not nice about her financial gifts. She always says, "because Chip would have wanted you to have it." Chip was her mother's husband. Angie's not sure exactly how much money her mother has but it's a lot.

Angie says she might like to start a business. She's a practical person, good with details.

"Eunice did that, remember?" Sam asks. Eunice was another aide at Lindell. She's older than they are, in her late fifties. She started a home care agency. Angie hears it's doing well.

"I'd rather run a store, sell something," Angie says.

"Like what?"

"I don't know. Books. I could open a bookstore."

"Dunston's full of readers. I guess college towns usually are."

Sam says she needs to go, she has a paper to finish for class tomorrow.

"On what?" Angie asks.

"The Romantic Poets."

"Ick."

"What, ick? You should read some Lord Byron. Shelley's good, too."

On her way out, Sam says she and Matt should come for dinner next week. She'll text her after she talks to Timothy.

After Sam leaves Angie considers the evening in front of her. Matt's at work until late; he'll stay the night with her. She gave him a key earlier so he could let himself in. She doesn't expect to be awake.

Now she thinks she won't be able to sleep. She'll be listening for him and watching the clock.

As a girl, she did that a lot. Her father would go out after dinner and return late. Sometimes he didn't come home at all. Her mother walked the floor until she wore herself out. The morning after was choked with silent gloom. Either her father would stumble in and say he was taking the day off work, or he'd struggle up off the couch where he'd thrown himself in the early hours.

Angie crawls into bed and watches an old movie. When it ends, she watches another one. She wakes up with a jolt, the television still on. It's after three a.m. and Matt's not there! She gets up, pulls on her bathrobe, and marches to the living room to find her phone. Peggy lifts her head from where she's nestled at the end of the bed but stays where she is. She knows it's too early for breakfast. The phone's not in the kitchen, the living room, or the bathroom. What the hell? Then Angie finds it on the nightstand, where she always keeps it, and in her fluster didn't think to look first.

She'd turned her notifications off so she wouldn't be disturbed. Even so, there are no texts or voice messages.

She sits on the edge of the bed and puts her head in her hands. The plot unfolds. He's still at the bar, handling an emergency; he's on his way, just got held up by something—or someone. The ex-girlfriend? Angie relives every moment they spent together, looking for the dark seed that sprouted while she slept. Is there *anything* genuine about him? Is he all talk? But Timothy likes him, right? They've been friends for a while now. And her dad liked him, too. What about Sam? She's a good judge of character. Sam has never said a thing, one way or another. Trying to spare her feelings? Doesn't want to interfere? Angie starts to punch in Sam's number then recalls the hour. Only a crazy person would bother someone this time of night.

She knows she won't be able to sleep, so she dresses, rubs Peggy's furry head for luck, and drives under a starless black sky to Matt's.

There's no one out. The traffic lights aren't on their usual pattern but flash red in all directions. Some houses have a single light on; most are dark.

His car is in his parking spot. There's light in the living room. The blinds are down but open, giving her a segmented view. Matt's there, standing, gesturing, clearly upset. A woman rises from the couch. Is this the ex? She doesn't look overweight. She paces then stands right in front of Matt. She points at him. Angie can hear nothing from inside her car. Should she park, get out, approach slowly, and hope something reaches her? Matt slashes the air with his hand in a clear gesture of refusal. The woman brings her hands together as if pleading. She's begging him to take her back? He won't because his heart now belongs to Angie?

She must have knocked on the door just as he was leaving for Angie's. Why did he even let her in? Is she the type to make a scene? Is she going to stalk him—and Angie—until she's ready to move on?

After Blake Rawls dumped her, Angie stopped going to class, but she was often on campus, waiting for him to pass along the walkway near his building; the cafeteria, where he usually ate alone; the Starbucks by the main library, where he told her it was over between them over a piping cup of hot chocolate. Once, she stood outside the closed door of his office when he was meeting with a student, a woman. He droned on about the challenges of social work, the problem of getting overly involved with one's clients, how one must never put one's heart on the line. Angie approached the door, certain that her blurred figure shadowed the frosted glass. He stopped talking, pushed his chair back, and got to his feet. When he came towards the door, Angie bolted. That was the end of her career as a stalker.

As she sits in her car, watching, Angie realizes she's stalking again. She should leave and try to get a few hours of sleep. She pulls forward far enough so she can turn around, then drives slowly back the way she came. As she passes the window, Matt and the woman are standing, holding each other, motionless.

By the time she gets home, her clenched jaw has become painful. She has composed about fifty farewell messages in her mind. Back inside, coat off, perched on her bed she types *Congratulations on getting back together with your gf* and doesn't hit send. He'll get one chance to explain, but of course, his story won't hold water, and that will be the end of their brief affair.

The gentle pressure of his hand on her shoulder wakes her. He's sitting on the bed, looking down at her. His face is quiet. He looks exhausted.

"Where the hell were you?" Angie asks. Her sleepiness softens her tone.

"Dealing with my sister."

"What?"

"She showed up at the bar right before closing time. I had no idea she was in town."

Angie sits up. When she picks up her phone, she learns that it's just before eight.

"Have you been up all night?" she asks.

"I grabbed a couple of hours."

"So, what happened?"

This sister—Jen—broke up with her boyfriend and left Pittsburgh. She hitchhiked the whole way. She says she's been clean for weeks. He knows she's lying. He's sure she's still using. She looks awful. He's never seen her so thin.

He said he didn't want to hear from her until she was really and truly clean, and would call the cops if she came around again. His voice is calm, and he speaks slowly, carefully. She takes his hand and asks him if she can get him anything. Maybe a cup of coffee?

67

He shakes his head.

"Maybe she can really pull herself out, this time," he says.

"She just might."

Angie wants to say that his sister must first decide that she wants to make a change. She has to decide she wants a life without drugs. Then she has to get the help she needs to make that a reality. After all of that, she has to stick to being clean, which means not hanging with people who aren't. She probably doesn't know anyone like that, except Matt and her mother. She has to find a new community, and she'll need help with that, too.

Matt must know all of this already, though. Saying so will only make him feel worse.

"Can I crash here for a while?" he asks. "I don't have to be at work until the early evening."

"Of course."

They'd had plans to check out a new bistro that just opened up, or feed the ducks down by the lake if the weather allowed. Angie gets out of bed and pulls back the covers on the other side so Matt can crawl in. He removes his jeans and shirt. Down to his boxers, he thumps onto the mattress. Angie tucks him in as if he were a child. He closes his eyes.

"I'm going to have a cup of coffee and a piece of toast. I'll be quiet, I promise."

He nods.

From the doorway, she blows him a kiss. His eyes are closed, and from the regular rhythm of his breathing, he's already asleep.

Her phone shows a recent missed call and a message. It's from Lynn Lowman. She says she's sorry to bother her on a Sunday, but she's been thinking about one of the interviews she conducted the Friday before, not one Angie sat in on, and she hopes she doesn't mind that she did one without her—her boss, what's her name, Sherry, said it was at okay. Anyhow, the lady she was with was talking about her past (of course she was, that was a dumb thing to say) and she said something weird, and Lynn just doesn't know what to make of it. If Angie has a minute, can she give her a call?

"Oh, what a pain in the ass," Angie says.

She makes her coffee and toast and enjoys them in the living room where the light is flowing through the large picture window. Peggy's on the floor, soaking up the warmth. Angie doesn't call Lynn back. Instead, she picks up the book she's been reading, a simple-minded romance that nonetheless keeps her engaged, and dives back in. Yet, thoughts of the night before intrude. Matt could have called. It would have taken no time and saved her a lot of heartache. But he was having a lot of heartache of his own, right? And he's here now, dreaming away in her bed.

Slowly, a sense of peace descends.

chapter seven

Lynn asks if she can close the door to Angie's office. Angie says she usually keeps it open, so people feel free to drop in. Lynn sits, pulls her chair close to Angie's desk, and leans forward, speaking so quietly that Angie has to lean forward, too.

"Lillian Firestone," Lynn says.

"What about her?"

"She's the one I called you about."

"Okay."

"She said when she was eleven years old, she killed her sister."

Angie rises, closes the door, and sits back down. "Go on."

Lynn asked her to describe the most significant time in her life. Lillian took a moment to think, talked a little about her marriage of over fifty years; then touched on her career as a pediatrician, something she pursued because her own sister had died when she only two. Lynn assumed the sister had died of an illness, and Lillian said nothing to the contrary. Then she said that she'd drowned her in the bathtub.

"Whoa," Angie says.

"I asked her to elaborate."

"I should think so."

Lillian admitted to a bad case of sibling rivalry. She was nine when the sister was born. She loved being an only child, *the* only child. The baby was frail for the first few months, and her parents monitored her closely. Before the baby's birth, they had done their best to prepare Lillian for the new arrival, and she looked forward to being an older sister. That all changed when she was eclipsed. She wasn't allowed to touch the baby without washing her hands. When she got a mild cold, she was ordered to stay away. Where she'd been the unrivaled center of attention, she was now banished.

"Maybe I should just listen to the recording myself," Angie says.

"I deleted it."

"Why?"

"Well, isn't it incriminating?"

"Only if it's true."

"You don't think it's true?"

Honestly, Angie doesn't know. How can she? How can anyone?

"Okay, what else did she say?" Angie asks.

Lillian felt herself change. She'd been loving before, even sweet. She became withdrawn, sullen, prone to outbursts of tears and angry words often aimed at the baby. Her parents—her father in particular—admonished her harshly.

One day her parents had friends over. The baby was asleep in the room she shared with Lillian—the house was small, with only two bedrooms. Her parents had promised her that some arrangement would be made, perhaps an addition would be built, that would give Lillian back her privacy, but nothing was ever done about it.

On the day the friends visit Lillian's mood is especially black. These are people her parents have known for years. They send Lillian a card on her birthday; usually a gift from them rests under the Christmas tree. That day they breeze past her to stand silently and marvel at the baby, before returning to the living room where drinks are served, cards played, all in an atmosphere of hushed and joyous wonderment.

Lillian stands by the crib, looking down at the sleeping child. She admits to herself that she—Dorothy—is beautiful. She sees why people compare babies to angels. The baby stirs, opens her pretty blue eyes, and focuses on Lillian. Will she fuss? Cry for their mother? Lillian pulls back the crocheted blanket, takes one ankle in each hand, and lifts her. She holds her upside down. Dorothy's face registers confusion, but no alarm. She came into the world upside down, after all. It probably doesn't feel that strange. Her face reddens as the blood rushes to her head. Her legs stiffen, she's about to wail. Lillian puts her back in the crib, wraps her in the blanket, then lifts her a second time and holds her the way she's been taught but never allowed to try. Dorothy feels meaty and solid in her arms. Lillian carries her out to the adults. "Look who's awake," she says. Their mother quickly takes the baby from Lillian in a clear gesture of rescue. Does she know what Lillian did only moments before? Can she read the malice in her mind?

"So, the child died what, a year and a half later?" Angie asks.

"Roughly."

"It was all decades ago. How can we be sure her memory is accurate?"

"I found her pretty sharp."

It's true. Lillian Firestone is one of the few residents over the age of ninety who maintains a clear focus on things.

"What about the death itself?" Angie asks.

The parents have a fight, about what Lillian doesn't know. They're not the kind of people who are open about things like that. The mother draws a bath for Dorothy, then returns to her angry husband. Lillian thinks she'll take over then, give Dorothy her bath, let her parents deal with the conflict. Dorothy is reluctant, then in the throes of the terrible twos, but Lillian overpowers her easily. She gets her in the tub. Her parents are shouting, where before they'd spoken tensely but at a normal volume. It occurs to Lillian just how much trouble Dorothy has caused by being alive. Their parents never fought like that before she came along. Lillian herself is still relegated firmly to second place, second best. It's so easy just to push her under the water and hold her still. She struggles, but to no avail. Lillian can't look

72

at her open eyes—that's too much, even for her. Her hand is over her heart and she feels its last beat. She leaves the bathroom without turning off the water. Doing so would have given away her presence there. She doesn't really know how much time passed before her mother recalls the drawn bath. Maybe the tub filled, and water flowed over the sill into the hallway. That part Lillian doesn't remember.

"Oh my god," Angie says.

"Yup."

"Where did all this happen?"

"Right here in Dunston. She's a local."

"It just seems impossible."

"You're still saying she's making it up?" Lynn's flushed. Her eyes shine with the drama of the story she's just shared.

"Oh, I don't know."

Angie tells Lynn to continue with her interview schedule. She'll go have a word with Lillian herself.

"Are you going to confront her?" Lynn asks.

"Of course not."

Lynn stands, smooths the front of her slacks, and leaves.

After lunch, Angie asks the nurse at the station in Lillian's wing if she can give them some time alone.

"Not bad news, I hope," the nurse says. Her name is Linda, and like Sherry, she's pushing 60. Lillian has two sons and a couple of grandchildren, and Linda's thoughts have obviously turned immediately to them.

"No, no bad news."

"She's watching TV."

"Perfect."

Angie knocks on the open door. Lillian stares at the screen in front of her. Angie says her name. It's only when she's inside the room and closes the door behind her that Lillian turns her head in her direction. With the remote control in her lap, she silences the TV.

Lillian gestures to the empty chair. It's her own, not Lindell's, with embroidered upholstery and a thick, comfortable seat.

"I've been expecting you," Lillian says. On the TV a man swings a golf club on an emerald green under a clear blue sky.

Angie falters; words don't come.

"You're here about my confession," Lillian says.

"Ms. Lowman shared some details of your interview."

"Those details being the murder of my sister."

"Yes."

Angie says she knows that with the passing of time, one's understanding of something that happened long ago might change. Events can be altered or misremembered.

"I'm not crazy," Lillian says. Her hair is silver, not white. She wears it in a bun secured with several large pins decorated with tiny seed pearls. She's a large woman, with broad shoulders. She would have been formidable in her youth, even at the age when she says she did the deed.

"I'm not suggesting you are," Angie says.

"It's your duty to print my interview."

"That's not possible."

"You *must*."

Angie pauses. She has to tread carefully.

"Have you spoken of this to anyone else? Your children perhaps? Your late husband?" Angie asks.

"No one."

74

"But why now?"

"I've been needing to unburden myself for a long time, so when I was asked to review my life, this rushed to the forefront."

"I see."

"You don't believe me."

"Well, it's not an easy thing to believe, is it?"

Lillian asks her to hand her the box on the closet shelf. It's old, covered in embossed red leather. The top bears the initials *LF.* Lillian says the box was a wedding present from her husband. She always kept things, even as a young woman, letters, recipes, locks of hair from their children; photographs of favorite places, but only a few of people; sketches she attempted during a mad artistic phase before she settled on medicine as a career.

It takes only a moment to remove what she's looking for. She hands the paper to Angie. It's a birth certificate for a Dorothy Firestone, born eighty-odd years before.

"This proves only that she was born, not that you killed her," Angie says.

"What other proof could there be now, except for my own statement?"

"Statement?"

"I intend to make a statement to the police."

"Lillian, really, I—"

"There is no statute of limitations on murder."

Angie massages her forehead to ease a rising pain. Lillian, while still strong, can't get to the police station without help, so in all likelihood, the police would have to come to her. Their presence on the premises might be upsetting to the other residents.

"Would you have said anything if Lynn hadn't interviewed you?" Angie asked.

Lillian stares at the TV. The box in her lap slips to one side as she shifts in her chair. She rights it.

"Most assuredly not. But this is my chance, and I'd be a fool not to take it," Lillian says.

"Chance for what?"

"My just desserts."

Angie offers to put the box away. Lillian wants to keep it with her for now. Angie says she'll be in touch. She's very glad to leave the room.

She knows she should talk to Sherry, bring her up to speed, but just can't. Maybe if she says nothing, nothing more will happen. If Lillian contacts the police, they'll probably just think she's some old lady with dementia.

The next morning, in her weekly therapy session, she tells Nancy all about Lillian. She is by turns animated, then pensive.

Nancy says Lillian clearly needs to unburden herself of something. She may—or may not—have committed the crime in question. What's important is that she *thinks* she has.

"I know all that," Angie says.

She leans back on the comfortable couch and considers the random nature of existence. What if the parents hadn't argued that day? Would Dorothy still be alive? Or would Lillian's hatred of her have come to the same conclusion months or even years later?

"She must have spent her whole life thinking about that one day, that one moment. I just can't imagine what that was like," Angie finally manages to say.

Nancy removes her thick glasses and pinches the top of her nose where their weight has left a mark. She puts the glasses back on and regards Angie.

"I suspect she put the incident from her mind. Suppressed it. That said, it would have always been there, informing her decisions, her outlook, in some form, I think."

"As in her deciding to become a pediatrician."

"Perhaps."

Angie knows people who commit a crime change the lives of their victims, but they also change their own lives forever. She's never considered this aspect before. When she was in the field, the abused women were her focus. The men she scarcely considered, except as monsters, things to be removed and punished. While she was able to consider their inner lives to the extent of finding a basis for violence, she didn't see them carrying their misdeeds with them into the future. To them, she imputed no regret or remorse.

This leads her down another path. She once thought desire drove every person forward; desire to have, desire to be rid of, but what if the results of a single deed were stronger still? You could live your entire life in the shadow of the misery you caused. It would reshape you entirely. The person you were before would disappear into the person you became afterward.

"Angie?"

"I'm just trying to figure out what to do about Lillian."

"Why not do as she asks? Contact the police."

Angie nods.

Nancy moves on. She wants to know how things are with Matt. Angie tells her about going to his apartment late Sunday night and seeing a woman he said was his sister in the window.

"You don't believe him?" Nancy asks.

"I don't know."

Angie considers the nice Sunday they had after he got enough sleep. She made him veal marsala. They shared a bottle of wine. He didn't mention his sister; Angie didn't bring her up, either. They took a walk after she did the dishes, though it was freezing out. He laughed at her wool hat, one she'd knit herself, and she wasn't upset. She knew it looked silly. Since talking to Lillian the day before she hasn't been in touch with him, although he's texted her twice. Soon he'll wonder what's going on, why she's not responding. Will he think it's because of something he's done? Will he worry that she's having second thoughts?

Nancy asks her to explore her reluctance to take him at face value.

"Maybe I'm just a skeptic," Angie says.

"Some skepticism is healthy."

"I think everyone's a liar."

"How about you?"

She's told her share of lies, but nothing big, like making up a murder, or saying an old girlfriend is really your meth monkey sister. When she was younger, she put a premium on honesty, which was often brutal for those she targeted. "You stink," she told more than one sibling more than once. "You walk like an old man," she told Timothy about a slight limp he'd always had and couldn't help. "You wasted your education," she told Foster. She felt a degree from an Ivy League school demanded more than a job in a vet's office. She was told her honesty was a weapon, a means to hand out judgment that was seldom unbiased. Her mother said she liked to beat people up with her words.

Angie keeps all this to herself.

"Maybe I figure if someone is lying to me, I don't have to take them seriously," she says.

"Like a protective barrier?"

"More or less."

Nancy reminds her that they recently touched on the topic of trust.

"I know, I know," Angie says.

Nancy asks how she feels about her job these days, quite apart from Lillian's startling story. Is she still cynical? Feeling burned-out? Angie pauses and considers that she started at Lindell steeped in the idea that everyone was a unique individual worthy of respect and high-quality care. She still thinks so, but over time the residents faded into the background, became featureless, lost some of their individuality. Guilt floods her. Does this happen to other people? Doctors, for instance, seeing patient after patient, year after year? Do those souls just become case notes? In trying to help others, do we lose sight of them?

She tells Nancy she's thinking about quitting, finding another career. It's not just a pipe dream, she's got the money to coast awhile if she's careful.

Nancy says they can expand on that next week because their time for today is up.

At Lindell, Angie goes straight to Sherry and unburdens herself about Lillian. Sherry isn't surprised. She's heard a lot of odd things over the years. A man once told her he tried to poison his wife, but what he slipped in her tea only made her ill for a little while. The wife suspected he was out to do her in, and although she couldn't prove it, she left him. He married again, and over fifty years later he and his second wife occupied one of Lindell's independent living cottages. There are other stories, less violent, but all suggesting long-standing hatreds and feuds.

"We all carry some bitterness around, don't we?" Sherry asks.

She's wearing a white blouse and a pink cardigan. Her face is gentle, kind, her eyes are bright and aware. Angie can't imagine what bitterness she lives with.

"I'll talk to her, confirm that she really does want to talk to the police, and then we'll proceed from there," Sherry says.

"But how can such a thing ever be proven?" Angie asks.

"I don't think it can. And I'm pretty sure the police will quickly come to that conclusion."

They sit for a moment.

Sherry asks her how it's going.

"Fine."

"You seem distracted. Is it just Lillian spilling the beans?"

"Really, everything's cool."

"Well, I don't mean to pry. I just hope you're still happy with us here. You're very valuable."

Angie has trouble seeing herself in that light. She's a functionary, shuffling paperwork, keeping track of the residents, soothing their anxious children. Just the week before a man called to say that his mother always sounds sad on the phone. Angie told him that what he perceives as sadness is probably just the normal emotional detachment of someone her age. Angie spent some time with her and got a smile or two. She called the son the following day to tell him this, and he said his mother was always one to put on a brave face.

"I'm always here if you need me," Sherry says, then turns to her computer screen, signaling that the meeting is over.

The day passes normally. Lynn is somewhere in the nursing wing, recording. She has three more days, and then she'll compile what she's gotten. Angie worries that something even more dire might come to light, then realizes that there's nothing more dire than murder.

She texts Matt and apologizes for taking so long to get back to him. She blames work. They're having dinner at Timothy and Sam's on Friday, and she says she's really looking forward to that.

I can come by the bar later if you like, she writes.

Thirty seconds later she sees *You bet!* on her screen.

He must be having a slow day, she thinks, then chides herself for that nasty sardonic voice that's her default setting.

chapter eight

Sam makes lasagna for the dinner party. The house smells wonderful and looks wonderful, too. There is a new painting on the wall, an abstract seascape. A short, sturdy rubber tree has been added to the nook by the French doors that lead to the back yard, now blanketed with six inches of last night's snow. The wood floors gleam, the hand-woven Peruvian rugs, bought at a crafts fair in Syracuse, make for a soothing, welcoming atmosphere.

Sam and Timothy are a great couple. They're open, supportive, and share everything. Words are sweetly said. They hold hands on the couch, watching TV. Tonight, though, some unspoken strain haunts them. They don't look each other in the eye.

Watching Sam and Timothy maneuver around the small galley-style kitchen without any physical contact puts Angie on edge. She has a keen nose for disaster. She was the first to realize her parents were through. It helped that she was the eldest, and was that much more aware of the sad meanderings of their adult lives than her siblings, but she's certain her sense of people is just sharper. She's a good observer. She picks up on things fast.

Matt's still upset about his sister and tells the story to Sam and Timothy. Sam commiserates. Timothy says it truly sucks. Matt sits at the kitchen counter, slowly twirling his bottle of beer. He's wearing a long-sleeved turtleneck, torn jeans, and hiking boots. Sam and Timothy are both in jeans and flannel shirts. Angie's in tailored slacks and a silk button-down blouse. She wore something less nice to work, went home, and changed. Who is she trying to impress? No one's commented on her appearance.

When Matt winds down, an uneasy silence falls. Timothy sits at the counter now, too. Sam's hovering by the stove, though her dish isn't due to come out of the oven for another twenty minutes. Angie's by herself in the living room, only a few feet away, but Sam's strategic furniture placement has made the space its own, clearly separated from the kitchen.

The men, with their backs to Angie, talk. Timothy draws Matt out again about his sister. Matt shakes his head and drinks more beer. Sam leaves the kitchen, and as she walks around the end of the counter where the occupied stools are set, Timothy reaches out his hand. She brushes it with her own but doesn't look at him.

Peace offering? Desperate plea?

Sam joins Angie. Her expression is less hard than before as if stubbornness has been replaced with fatigue. Angie looks at her questioningly.

"I'm supposed to see my father this weekend," Sam says.

"And you don't want to?"

Sam's sigh signals her ambivalence. Matt turns on his stool and looks at her.

"Put him in the picture," Timothy says.

"He won't want to hear," Sam says.

"Try me," Matt says.

Angie's heard most of it before, but the retelling makes it new.

Growing up, Sam was told her mother had been raped, and the rapist, then living in another town, died young. To call it a fanciful tale was an understatement. The truth was that her mother was involved with the father romantically, and learning of her pregnancy, he offered to marry her. He wanted to. He was in love with her. Sam's grandparents were the strictest sort of religious fanatics, declaring that their daughter was a sinner and beyond redemption. Even when the father—Henry—came to the house to plead his case, Sam's mother turned him away. She'd been raised with the weight of guilt and failure always on her and was so accustomed to being thought ill of that she couldn't conceive of happiness, even when given the chance. Henry went away to college, returned to town, and married someone else. He had three children, but he put money aside for Sam for the day she reached out to him, or he died, whichever came first.

One day her mother came clean. She'd read in the paper that Henry's father had been killed in an accident. There was money in the family, and Sam's mother assumed that Henry would soon come into a healthy inheritance. Her miserable parents had been in the ground for years by then, and she'd slowly found herself in their absence. After rejecting Henry's repeated offer of financial help after Sam was born, she now wanted her share. Sam was to get it for her. Sam refused, but she did go to see him. That's when she learned of his investment and how much it had grown. She could have it on a moment's notice, as long as she understood the tax consequences involved.

He lives only blocks away, but they're seldom in touch. She'd met her half-sister and two half-brothers several Christmases before, and was ill at ease with them, though they seemed kind enough. Now one of the brothers is getting married, and Sam's invited to the wedding. Timothy is urging her to accept.

"Will you?" Matt asks.

"I don't know."

"You treat them like the plague," Timothy says.

To Angie's surprise, Sam laughs.

"I do, don't I?" Sam asks.

She says the problem is that she's too used to thinking of herself as an only child. She doesn't know how to fit them in.

"Well, consider them as an extended family. Like distant cousins," Angie says.

"Maybe."

Sam offers Angie another glass of wine. Angie accepts and relaxes into the couch. The evening's mood lightens.

A few minutes later the food comes out, rests, and they all convene at the small dining table in the bay window, overlooking the yard. Sam asks how Angie's week was, and Angie tells her about Lillian Firestone. Matt's fork stops on the way from his plate to his mouth and he says, "Whoa, you didn't say anything about that."

"I was still trying to process it," Angie says.

Timothy asks if she called the police on Lillian's behalf. Angie says her boss did that.

"Poor old lady, trying to alleviate her guilt," Sam says.

Angie says that guilt is a powerful motivation. Three years before, when her mother's second husband died suddenly, her mother was up to her ears in it.

"She wondered if she'd ever really loved him," Timothy tells Matt.

"And did she?" Matt asks.

"As much as she loved anyone, I think," Angie says, not unkindly.

Timothy meets her eye. Their mother is a tough person, and affection doesn't come easily for her. This trait shows in Timothy as trying too hard to be loving, though love clearly comes naturally to him. He's just afraid that one day it might not, Angie thinks. For her, she knows she has inherited a natural harshness towards people that keeps them at arm's length. Thinking this, she looks at Matt, wondering if he senses that in her, or if she's been successful so far in hiding it. He's working away on his lasagna and doesn't see her watching him.

"Do you think it's true, what Lillian told you?" Sam asks.

"I really don't know."

"Look into it," Sam says.

"How?"

"Ask her family."

85

"That's awkward. 'Hi, I'm Angie Dugan, a social worker at your mom's retirement home, and she says she killed her baby sister eighty years ago. Do you know anything about that?'"

"Stranger things must have happened," Matt says. He's cleaned his plate.

"No doubt." Angie leans back, her sour mood returning. She shouldn't have said anything about Lillian to anyone, including Sherry. She thinks now it's all nonsense, just a way for Lillian to get some attention.

Timothy asks Matt what's new at the bar since the coke bust. Matt says his boss didn't get charged, and that his lawyer might sue the police for false arrest. Sharon's not so lucky. She might have to do time. She's pretty worried about it. She's been calling him every day, asking for advice.

"What advice can you give her now, except that she shouldn't have been dealing?" Angie asks.

"She just needs to talk."

"To you?"

"Sure. Aren't I a good listener?"

This puts a nasty spin on things that makes Angie shift around in her chair before sitting still once again.

"You're a *great* listener," Angie says, hoping she sounds genuine.

Sam stands and clears away the plates.

Timothy asks when the bar is going to have live music again.

"Soon. I gave the green light to a new metal band in town after I listened to some of their stuff," Matt says.

"Why was it up to you?" Angie asks.

"The boss was dealing with the arrest thing. But I wouldn't mind choosing all the time if he'd let me."

"You could ask him," says Sam, running water in the sink.

Angie sees Matt thinking about it. Maybe he doesn't have enough confidence.

She could encourage him. Why doesn't she? Because she's upset by how close he and Sharon actually are? He never talks about her. Because he doesn't want to give away his real feelings for her? Or because in fact, he doesn't think it's worth mentioning?

"You okay?" Matt asks her.

"Sure."

Timothy catches Sam's eye in the kitchen. Sam nods. She asks Matt if he minds giving her a hand. Matt's happy to. Timothy invites Angie back into the living room where he lights a fire. Angie watches the flames rise, trying to lose her thoughts in them. She wishes Matt had told her about the calls from Sharon before. She doesn't like being blind-sided when other people are around. It limits how she can respond. But had they been alone, she probably wouldn't have said much about it anyway, not until she'd had a chance to really think it all through.

"Listen," Timothy says. "I need to talk to you about Dad."

"Yeah?"

"He's drinking again."

"More than usual?"

"A lot."

Angie rubs her forehead. The other night at his house there'd been no sign. He might have been drinking before she got there. She knows he's good at hiding it.

Timothy says there's trouble between him and Mary Beth. He thinks there's someone else, someone Mary Beth met through work. He's pretty sure their dad knows about it, too. Angie asks him why.

"Because of something he said a couple of weekends ago."

Timothy had gone over to watch the Saints-Packers game. Mary Beth was out, which he thought unusual for a Sunday. Potter said she had to meet a homeowner because that was the only time the guy was free for the next few weeks. It was the way he said it as if he'd just remembered, which meant he'd been thinking about it all day.

Did Angie remember how he used to talk about their mother that way? Yes, she did. And she really hoped history wasn't repeating itself. If it were, she'd brain Mary Beth, something she's always wanted to do, by the way.

Timothy agrees. Mary Beth has never been his favorite.

"So, how do you know he's drinking more?" Angie asks.

"I walked past the recycle bin in the garage on my way out. It had about five or six empty bourbon bottles."

Timothy says Mary Beth doesn't include him in her work anymore. Potter was a sort of client liaison until a few weeks ago, walking customers through their design options, soothing their frustrations when things didn't happen fast enough. He's not sure what happened exactly. All Potter would say was that he'd been furloughed.

Angie wonders if he were drinking on the job. It wouldn't be the first time. Dunston is full of small businesses that had to let him go for that very reason. Years ago he kept a flask in his back pocket. Then he used a thermos that had spiked coffee. After that, he bought plastic bottles of water, emptied them, and filled them up with gin. The trouble was he hated gin and forcing himself to choke it down made him even more unpredictable with strangers. Once, when he was a clerk at Johnson's Hardware, he told a customer she reminded him of a cat. He meant it as a compliment, but she threw the paint cards she'd been looking out in his face and stormed out. Another time he urged a little boy to go pull his sister's hair, saying it was the right of every brother on earth to do that. The girl's howl was shockingly loud. The finger the boy pointed at Potter doomed him to another firing. And now, with free time on his hands and a cheating wife on his mind, how long can he hold on?

"Have you talked to him?" Angie asks.

"You know I'm no good at that."

Angie has always been able to reach him but doesn't want to do it alone this time. Could she enlist his sister, Patty, in Montana to make a phone call? No, it would be too easy for him to hang up. The only other person who could ever make him listen is Angie's mother, Lavinia. Asking her to reach out could backfire, but then Angie thinks not. Her mother has mellowed. She's into gardening and her book club. She might even bring a degree of kindness to bear.

She tells Timothy she'll handle it and report back. He's visibly relieved.

"Have you talked to the others about it?" Angie asks, meaning the twins and Foster.

"No."

"Good. Let's keep this to ourselves for now."

They both know this means until and unless their father goes completely off the rails.

Matt and Angie came in separate cars. He follows her back to her place. He asks what the big talk with Timothy was about. Angie's pretty sure he could hear most of it but tells him anyway.

"Man. My sister, your dad," he says.

Angie softens. She loves that he sees this connection between them. Relationships are all about having things in common. In this case, they share a kindred unhappiness. She wishes they can find positive ground and hopes they will in time.

chapter nine

Lillian Firestone's file lists a son living in Dunston. Angie hesitates, though she's prepared her introduction many times. Talking to a resident's family members doesn't usually make her nervous, not since she first came to work here. Since then she's developed a bland, pleasant tone that seems to put people at ease. It's that tone she adopts when Jared Firestone answers the phone.

After reassuring him that his mother's health has not suddenly declined, she says she would like to meet. She has something she needs to discuss, and the telephone just feels too awkward. He sounds apprehensive. She promises him it's nothing serious, then wonders what he'll say when he realizes she lied through her teeth.

He says he could come out to Lindell. Angie suggests she come to him if that's convenient. He pauses. He's an artist and works in his studio most days. She can come there if she likes. He gives her the address which matches what the file has.

She lets the receptionist out front know she can be reached on her cell phone. The receptionist is a sixteen-year-old high school dropout, a resident's granddaughter, and has trouble keeping information straight though she tries hard. Angie watches her note Angie's departure time in the sign-in book. After writing the wrong date, she erases it and writes in the correct one. Angie doesn't tell her that the sign-in book is for visitors, not staff. She'll get around to it one of these days.

Jared's studio is way out in the country, south of Dunston. The dairy farms of Angie's youth are still there. A side road leads to the house her father and Aunt Patty grew up in. Years ago, when it was old and abandoned, Patty bought it back from the man their father sold it to. She wanted to remodel it and sell it for a good price. Potter did the work until the guy working with him got drunk and failed to douse the charcoal grill he was cooking on. A tarp caught fire, and the whole place went up. Angie had been out with Potter having dinner, and driving home afterward they saw the sky was full of smoke. Potter seemed to know at once where it was coming from. The color drained from his face, and his jaw turned hard and square.

That memory, coupled with the darkening sky that says more snow is on the way, makes Angie sad.

Jared's house is not far back from the road, but the studio is about a quarter-mile farther. Angie comes to what looks like another house, smaller than the first, with three stairs up, a front porch, a tall window on either side of the door, painted dark green. The brass knocker looks new. Before she can use it, Jared opens the door and ushers her quickly inside to keep the heat from escaping. He's well over six feet tall, which makes him seem to take up most of the small room. He's in his mid-sixties, with salt and pepper hair and a fierce look in his blue eyes which reminds Angie at once of Lillian. He wears a denim shirt and jeans, both of which are paint-splattered. He shakes her hand; his palm is rough. He says he was just about to make coffee if she'd care for some. She says she's fine. On one wall there's a counter with a two-burner stove, a sink, and small refrigerator underneath, the kind you'd find in a college dorm room. There's a door that must lead to a bathroom. Jared's easel is at the other end, next to a wood stove. Two easy chairs are arranged to one side. He gestures for Angie to take one. She does.

He stands by his easel, picks up a brush, and considers the canvas before him, all grey and white swirls. The smell of brewing coffee comforts her. She leans back, much more at ease.

"What has my lantern-jawed mother been up to now?" he asks. His tone is neither affectionate nor hostile.

"Well, it's a bit odd actually," Angie says. She describes the folklore project and what Lynn Lowman told her. She says she spoke to his mother herself afterward.

Jared puts down his brush and stares at Angie.

"Say that again," he says.

Angie repeats the essential point.

"Well, well," he says.

"You don't sound very surprised."

"I wouldn't say that. Mother is a strange creature, always was, capable of deep feelings, more than most people, I mean. She's also very strong-willed. She kept her maiden name long before it was popular to. My father objected to that, and to a lot of things she did. Their marriage was often stormy."

"She was a pediatrician."

"Yes, and surprisingly her menacing nature never made it into the examination room."

Menacing nature?

Angie asks him to clarify.

"She was hard on me and my brother. Demanding. Not terribly loving, but not altogether unkind, either. She didn't believe in coddling."

He steps away to pour out some coffee for himself.

"Is there any truth to what she said?" Angie asks.

"Oh, I'm certain there's not."

"But how can you be sure?"

"I'm her son."

Angie knows not to press him. She asks about his work. She says she thinks she's heard of him, although she hasn't, and he looks pleased. He studied abroad when he was younger and worked in New York City for a while, but the rolling hills of Upstate eventually called him home. He speaks of a man named Frank who died several years before, which was when he decided to move back. Angie infers that this was a gay partner, but detects no grief in Jared's demeanor at the mention of his name.

"My sister is a painter," Angie says.

"Really?"

"Pastels and oils mostly."

"Lovely."

Jared wipes his brush on a rag. He seems unhappy with his canvas as if thinking it needs something more. To Angie's eye, it's awfully quiet, almost dull. Jared puts down the brush and chooses a narrower one, with fewer bristles.

"How do you like working at Lindell?" he asks.

"Oh, it has its ups and downs. I like the residents."

"What would you say is the best part of your job?"

Angie has to think about that for a moment.

"Drawing someone out, helping him get involved in something."

"But some just want to be left alone."

"Yes."

Jared dips his brush into a tiny jar of deep blue paint and presses the brush in the middle of the canvas. Angie looks hard and decides the dot of color is only an idea and doesn't change the impression overall.

"You mustn't worry too much about what my mother says. I know it's startling, but I think she'll let the matter go," he says.

"My boss called the police. They came to talk to her."

Jared sips his coffee, then puts the mug back on the floor by his feet.

"That must have been quite an interview," he says.

"I don't think they stayed very long."

"No, I imagine not."

Angie thanks him for his time and says she has to get back.

"I appreciate your coming to see me. You're right. This would have been a very awkward phone call."

As she drives snow falls. Angie replays her meeting with Jared. Either he's a great faker, and was actually shocked as hell, or he was being honest when he said the whole thing wasn't a big deal.

She tells Sherry she talked to Lillian's son and didn't learn anything new. For a moment Sherry doesn't seem to know what Angie's referring to, then focusses. She says she's heard nothing more. The police haven't been in touch since they came out, and Lillian is just her usual self, though she's complaining more about what the dining room serves. Angie should talk to the kitchen staff and see if a slight menu change can be made. This isn't strictly Angie's job, but then so many things aren't, like buying a new pair of swim trunks for Mr. Peterson who decided recently to avail himself of Lindell's indoor pool to do some laps; or making an appointment with a hairstylist downtown for Marjorie Miller after she declared that the long hair she'd worn all her life had to go.

Angie swings by Lorna Green's room to see how her first couple of weeks at Lindell have gone. The memory care wing is quiet, except for soft classical music drifting from the overhead speakers. Lorna sits at a folding table, staring at some colored pencils and a pad of paper. An aide is with her, encouraging her to draw something that makes her happy. The aide is another new hire, Bethany. Her pop-culture name is echoed in her glue-on nails and hair streaked with green. Lorna can't manage the pencils. She says she would like some chocolate to give Danny when he comes home from school. Then she says she's cold. The room is stifling. Angie gets her a blanket from the closet and drapes it awkwardly around her shoulders. The visit depresses her, and she leaves without saying another word to either Lorna or Bethany.

On a whim, Angie swings by Matt's bar after work. It's Thursday, a football game plays on the TV mounted on the wall. There are only a handful of customers. The atmosphere feels hollow. She needs to kill time before her mother comes over after dinner. Lavinia doesn't know what Angie's going to lay on her, and Angie has a bad feeling about how she'll react. She sits at the bar and sees at once that Matt's not here. Jackson, a co-worker, is on duty. Jackson's a college kid with a buzz cut. Angie recalls him saying he was majoring in Philosophy.

She asks him where Matt is.

"Not sure. He got a call and said he had to leave."

"Oh, will he be back?"

"Hope so. Might get busy later."

Angie asks for a beer. Jackson brings it and wants to know if she's going to order any food. Angie shakes her head. She didn't tell Matt she was coming. In her last text to him that day she said she was going straight home to deal with her mother. It wouldn't have occurred to him that she'd suddenly change her mind. He mentioned he was going to join a gym and start using weights again. Maybe that's where he went, but in the middle of a shift? No, this was something that just came up.

"Hey, have you seen Sharon around lately?" Angie asks Jackson.

"Not since she quit. Got fired. Left, whatever."

Angie looks at her watch. Her mother's not due for another hour. Peggy's used to late dinners, so Angie settles in and concentrates on enjoying her beer. As bothered as she is by Matt's unexplained absence, her mind turns back to Jared Firestone. There's something he's not telling her. But whatever it is doesn't matter. Lillian may or may not have killed her sister. In any case, nothing is going to come of it.

Did confessing ease her mind? Over the years, how often did she think back to the one day, so long ago? Did it haunt her, or did she get used to living with the guilt? Maybe she felt no guilt until recently. Maybe she let herself off the hook. She might have felt justified. A person can rationalize anything if they try hard enough.

For Angie, rationalization often takes the form of accepting another person's lame excuses, which at the time she calls plausible explanations. She did a lot of that with her boyfriend, Brett, when he didn't pay his share of the rent, buy groceries, or take her out to eat. He said his parents kept him on a tight leash financially so he would persist in his studies and not be frivolous. His racy sports car always made her wonder, and she told herself it was probably a gift from them before they turned off the money spigot. Then he'd come home with a new jacket or a really nice pair of shoes and say he had a credit card he hadn't quite maxed out yet. After she met Jerry at Lindell and they went out a couple of times, she told herself his neediness was a form of flattery. She knew deep down he was just reeling from his mother's death and his recent divorce. She won't do that with Matt. He's going to have to be completely straight with her.

She calls his number and it goes right to voice mail. Who is he talking to? Why would he leave to meet someone and then jump on the phone?

Because she's late and he wants to know where she is.

Stop it!

She pays for her beer and stands up. Matt comes through the door, flushed. He sees her right away and closes the distance quickly.

"What are you doing here?" he asks and kisses her on the cheek.

"I just dropped in."

"Sorry I was out."

"Yeah, Jackson said you had to leave."

"My mom called, and I didn't want to talk to her here, so I walked around the Commons."

"In this cold?"

"Right? I'm freezing."

He takes off his insulated jacket and puts it on a hook in a little hall that leads to the storeroom.

"What did she want?" Angie asks, aware that Jackson is within earshot, as are a couple who just claimed two barstools.

"I'll tell you later." They stand, looking at each other. Angie doesn't remember Matt being so tall, then remembers she's wearing flats.

"Did you see your mother already?" he asks.

"No, going there now."

"Let me know how it goes."

"Okay."

Angie sinks. The short drive home is difficult. She wants to go to bed tonight and wake up as someone different, a woman who doesn't suspect, a woman who trusts.

Nancy's going to have a field day with that one.

As she turns onto her road, she realizes there's nothing in the house to eat except a carton of eggs and a loaf of bread. She was supposed to go to the store that afternoon and forgot. Her lunch was light, a wilted salad from the dining room. Her stress level will result in a few lost pounds. It always does. Thin and miserable versus fat and happy? But she's never happy. When was the last time she was?

Her mother's car is in the driveway. She's let herself in with the key Angie gave her after her step-father died. She's never made use of it before today. Angie's thought at the time was that her mother might need a break from the large empty home she inherited, presumably while Angie was at work. Seeing her perched on the couch comfortably with Peggy in her lap, Angie checks her phone, which shows two missed calls from her mother's number. She doesn't remember turning off the ringer.

"You're early," Angie says.

"Hope you don't mind."

Lavinia's lost weight again. Her chin is pointed, her eyes large and probing. The turtleneck sweater she wears does little to hide the bony silhouette of her shoulders. Her wrists, decorated with bangles and gold chains are so frail Angie imagines them snapping if she slipped and fell on an icy sidewalk.

Angie sits down in her favorite chair without removing her coat. She says she went to see her boyfriend.

"Since when?" Lavinia asks. Angie doesn't remember if she's mentioned Matt to her or not, then realizes she hadn't. Angie fills her in, leaving out the part about not believing a word he says.

Angie wriggles out of her coat and remains sitting. She looks at Peggy.

"I need to feed her," she says.

"I did that. She was yowling like mad when I got here."

"Thanks."

Lavinia has managed to find Angie's good bottle of French wine. She's consumed half of it already. She never drank when Angie was growing up. She didn't drink much during the run of her second marriage, either, though she did get arrested for driving under the influence. Angie only learned of that recently. There was a time when Lavinia would have been embarrassed and said nothing. She mentioned it out of the blue a couple of weekends ago when Angie and Timothy took her out to lunch and Timothy said one of his co-workers spent the night in jail for the same reason. She admitted to having slammed it back pretty hard that day, though she didn't say why. There seems to have followed a long period of moderation. Since losing her husband, she drinks daily, sometimes more than she should, kept company in that by Alma. Angie pours herself a glass. The first sip reminds her she's hungry.

"You don't want to grab a bite somewhere, do you?" she asks.

"I ate earlier."

That probably means a late breakfast consisting of a piece of toast and an apple.

"All I've got is bread and eggs."

"I can work with that. Scrambled or fried?"

"Scrambled."

Lavinia's on her feet quickly and goes into the kitchen around the corner. The sound of the frying pan being put on the stove and the refrigerator door opening and closing is comforting.

After a moment Lavinia calls out, "So, what are we talking about, anyway?"

"Hold on."

Angie changes clothes in the bedroom. She needs the softness of sweatpants and her favorite sweater to deal with the matter at hand. When she returns Lavinia presents her with a plate of food. Angie eats right there in the living room, expecting her mother to make some cold remark about her having a perfectly good dining room table. Lavinia says nothing. The eggs are perfect, soft and buttery, with just a touch of salt. Childhood breakfasts come back, the food being the only pleasure of those daily gatherings.

With a full stomach, Angie hopes she can relax, but the idea of her father's plight gnaws. She pours out the rest of the wine into their two glasses, takes her plate to the kitchen, and returns.

"Listen, Dad's hitting the bottle pretty hard again. Timothy says Mary Beth is having an affair and that he knows," she says.

Lavinia closes her eyes in an expression of sudden, devasting grief. Angie has never doubted her mother's continuing love for her father, but this one moment proves how deep that love really is.

"She's an awful woman," Lavinia says.

"I never liked her."

Lavinia removes a cigarette from the pack in her purse and lights it without asking Angie if she minds. Angie didn't know her mother smoked. She never did before. When she caught Angie smoking as a teenager, the punishment she doled out was harsh. No television or telephone privileges for an entire month. Plus having to do all the housework during that time. Angie knows her mother was both trying to teach her a lesson and earn herself a well-deserved break from the duties she performed without any help from her husband.

"What do you want me to do?" Lavinia asks.

"Talk to him. I'll be there, too."

"I can handle it alone."

"No, I want to be there. We just need to figure out what we're going to say."

"That he should knock it the hell off."

"That never helped before."

Lavinia's nod concedes the point.

She says he always promised to dry up and often did. But when something went wrong, back he'd go. She supposes they're all like that, at least the really hardcore ones. Angie reminds her that he cleaned up his act a whole lot when he got together with Mary Beth. If he could do it then, he can do it now.

"He'll need a reason," Lavinia says.

"True."

They both know that logic doesn't work. Nor do threats or pleas. The change has to come from within. There has to be something he wants badly enough to really try.

Lavinia looks out the picture window where the snow is collecting on Angie's fence.

"Get him on the phone, ask him to come over. Don't tell him I'm here," Lavinia says.

"Now?"

"It's only a little past seven."

"What if Mary Beth objects?"

"To hell with her. Besides, I bet she's not even home."

Angie calls and Potter doesn't answer. Her message is cheerful and light, saying she was just thinking about him and hopes she'll hear from him soon.

"Should we go over there?" she asks.

"Not yet. Give him a chance to call back."

Lavinia knows not to rush in on him. He'll only turn defensive, or worse, sullen and then weepy.

She asks Angie to tell her more about Matt. Angie hesitates. She relates where he lives and works, that she met him through Timothy. Then she tells him about the sister.

Lavinia listens, smokes, shakes her head.

"You know, I went through a lot of heartache in my life, and I never cracked up, turned to drugs, lost my mind, or anything. Some people just aren't cut out for this world, are they?" She stubs out her cigarette in a small tin box she's brought with her for that very purpose. Angie again admires her mother's practical nature.

"Just don't be hard on him," Angie says, meaning her father.

"Why would I? It's no skin off my nose if he wants to get pickled."

"Okay."

"Don't worry, I won't tell him that. I'll just say he should act in his own best interest. That he can put that hag behind him if he really wants, and I'm sure he does. He never really loved her anyway."

"What? Why do you say that?"

"Do you have any more wine?"

"Yes."

The second bottle is a far inferior label, but Lavinia doesn't seem to care. Angie opens and pours. The wine is sharp, almost bitter. They drink it anyway.

Angie thinks of Matt, walking around the Commons, talking on his phone. She remembers the glad look on his face when he saw her in the bar. Her eyes prickle, a tear forms and rolls down her cheek.

"Oh, dear," Lavinia says. She puts down her wine glass, then takes Angie's gently out of her hand, too, puts it next to hers, and goes around the house looking for a box of tissues. When she can't find one, she goes into the bathroom and plucks some toilet paper from the roll. She stands by Angie's chair, stroking her hair. Angie lifts her hand as a request that she please stop. She feels exposed and vulnerable, and the show of affection only makes it worse.

Lavinia sits on the couch and resumes sipping her wine. Angie leans back in her chair and lets her arms fall limply.

"Is this about your dad?" Lavinia asks. Lavinia was never one for heart-to-heart talks, though she's accessible in her way, and a good listener when she tries. She's clearly trying now.

Angie shakes her head.

"Then what?"

Angie says she's scared to death.

"Of?"

"Matt."

"He sounds like a harmless enough sort. Of course, he's a man, and they're unpredictable creatures, though they no doubt say the same of us."

"He'll find out."

"What?"

"What I'm really like."

"And what are you really like?"

102

Angie gets up to use the bathroom. She inspects herself in the mirror. She looks awful, all puffy and blotchy as if she's been ill. She *feels* ill.

She returns to the living room where Lavinia has lit a fire.

"I'm not a nice person," Angie says.

"Says who?"

"Everyone."

"Specify."

Her siblings, for one.

"You were always hard on them, but they still love you," Lavinia says.

Angie reflects. Her mother's right.

"Would Matt be drawn to you if you weren't a nice person?" Lavinia asks.

"As I say, he doesn't really know me."

"Nonsense. You act like you've got some big terrible secret he's going to discover and then dump you."

She asks, but isn't that what always happens? Her mother says she needs to consider each case separately. Aside from Blake Rawls, Lavinia doesn't know much about the other two affairs. She only knows about Rawls because Angie was living at home then and took to her bed for two weeks when he said he didn't want to see her again.

Angie lays out the core details of her involvement with both Brett and Jerry. Lavinia sits, listening. Her body is taut as if she could spring up at any moment.

"They were the ones with secrets, not you. Brett was a rich kid playing a poor one, so you'd foot the bill. And he had a girl on the side you couldn't possibly have known about. Jerry was still in love with his ex-wife, which probably wasn't really a secret, just a lot harder on him than he realized."

103

"Maybe."

"Not maybe, definitely."

Peggy stretches on the couch next to Lavinia. The outside lights show another half-inch of snow on the fence. When Angie looks at her phone, she sees it's only been about twenty minutes since she called Potter. Misery has a weird way of warping time, she thinks. Einstein should have looked into that.

"Is it that you're afraid you can't love him back?" Lavinia asks.

"No!"

"It's nothing to be ashamed of. Loving someone is harder than most people assume."

Of course, her mother is right. Angie worries all the time if her heart is big enough for Matt—for anyone.

Even so, her entire life has been one long study in unrequited love. Has she confused longing for love? And what about lust? How does that figure in? Her head hurts. Maybe she's coming down with something.

"I feel lousy," Angie says. Lavinia stands and puts her palm on Angie's forehead.

"You're a little warm. You should go to bed."

"It's too early."

"Go on, scat. I'll do your dishes."

Angie does as she's told, grateful that her mother is taking charge. She brings her phone into the bedroom in case Potter calls. She knows he won't, not until tomorrow at the earliest. Lavinia sticks her head in to say the kitchen's all done, she's recorked the wine, and even let Peggy out for a last chance to do her business for the day. Is there anything she can get her before she heads home?

"No, I'm fine. And thank you for everything."

Lavinia blows her a kiss from the doorway. After she slams the front door behind her and the sound of her car has lessened and died away, Angie sees again that her mother isn't the same person she used to be.

chapter ten

Angie wakes early on Friday. She feels fine but can't face Lindell. She leaves a message for Sherry saying she's running a fever. She hasn't taken a sick day for almost a year, but staying home feels wrong. She's so conditioned to getting up and going to work that her vacation days have accumulated, too.

On her phone is a text message from Potter saying he's sorry he didn't pick up when she called. He hopes everything is okay. He obviously could hear her concern in the forced cheer of her recorded words.

Matt has also texted, wanting to know how the visit with Lavinia went. She texts back to say it went fine. He won't be up yet, so she doesn't expect a reply for a few more hours.

On her laptop, she finds an email from Lynn Lowman.

I've got some really great stuff here! Can't wait to share it with you!

No one's story is going to top Lillian's, so Angie can't imagine what Lynn is so excited about. She'll keep an open mind, though, and dutifully listen to what Lynn's recorded.

Lynn's note also says she'd like to connect over Facebook if that's okay.

Angie's email back just says, *Great!*

The day is bright; the snow glitters. What to do with the hours before her?

She cleans the house from top to bottom, even removing everything from the kitchen and bathroom cabinets. She pulls the books from the bookcase and dusts the shelves. The music she listens to is classical, a taste developed in college after visiting Blake Rawls in his office where a portable CD player offered the measured brilliance of Vivaldi. For once, she doesn't mind the memory of him, because she tells herself she got this one good thing out of the whole situation. She needs to consider what else she gained from her experiences with Brett and Jerry. When she can identify this, she will no doubt feel less bitter.

She moves fast and is done in about two and a half hours. She needs to get to the grocery store, but the thought is suddenly and inexplicably overwhelming.

She showers, dresses, and heads over to her mother's place. Even if she's not home, there will be food in the refrigerator. Her mother may eat like a bird, but Alma has a good appetite.

It occurs to her that this is a clear sign of regression and doesn't care. How long has she been looking out for other people? Can't someone watch out for her for a change?

Her phone rings and she answers, hoping some zealous Dunston police officer isn't out patrolling for distracted drivers. It's her sister in New York City, Marta, the sometimes actress.

"Hey, Dad called last night, and he sounded pretty out of it," she says.

"Yeah, he's going through a rough patch."

"A fifth of bourbon is more like it."

"What did he say?"

"He just wanted to know how Maggie and I are."

"And, how are you?"

"Dandy."

Their conversation is awkward because of their long-standing friction. Angie thinks both twins are pampered and spoiled; they think she's a needless hard-ass. The common ground they have always found is their parents or their other siblings.

"Why is he drinking again?" Marta asks. On her end, there's the sound of car horns. Angie doesn't like the city and only goes down when she tires of the shopping options in Dunston.

"Mary Beth."

"She's cheating on him?"

Angie admires how quickly Marta guessed the truth.

"Yes," Angie says.

"Shit. Poor dad."

"We're going to talk to him, see if there's anything we can do."

"Who's 'we?'"

"Mom and I."

"Oh, man. Is that a good idea?"

Angie reminds Marta that their mother knows Potter better than anyone. Plus, she still cares for him a lot.

"Well, good luck, and let me know what happens," Marta says.

"Will do."

The long curving driveway at her mother's house is steep enough for Angie's Toyota station wagon to have a little trouble maintaining traction, despite a new set of tires. Her mother drives a Land Rover that handles snow easily. If Alma complains about wheeling the garbage bins down through the muck, she calls someone to come out and plow it.

Coming up the walk to the back door Angie notices that a couple of bricks are cracked and crumbling. The paint around the windows is chipped, so is the paint on the door itself. The pane at the top of the door is dirty. She doesn't remember things looking like this the last time she was here, over the summer, but that kind of disintegration takes much longer to occur than just a few months. It startles Angie to realize her mother isn't paying attention to the shape the house is in because she used to obsess over it. When they all moved in there, almost twenty years before, the house was her pride and joy.

She goes inside. The kitchen is spotless and empty. Soft music plays from a distant room. She calls, "Hello?" and gets no reply, so she moves into the hallway and peeks into the empty dining room. The music is coming from the study. Alma's in there, lying on the couch reading a book. She sits up and stares at Angie.

"Well, look what the cat dragged in," she says, but there is warmth in her voice. Alma is almost 70 and doesn't get around as fast as she used to. When Angie and her siblings were younger, she was a terror. She went after all of them more than once with a broom, threatening to sweep them out the door if they didn't straighten up.

"Where's Mom?" Angie asks.

"Around here somewhere."

Angie removes her coat and throws it over the back of the couch. She sits in the chair on the other side of the marble-topped coffee table.

Alma asks why she isn't at work, and Angie says she needed a day off.

"Because of your dad?" Alma asks.

"She told you about that?"

"Timothy did too."

Angie's not really surprised. Alma's part of the family.

Alma asks if she would like a nice salami sandwich. It's only eleven, but Alma says she prefers an early lunch. They go into the kitchen. Angie doesn't like the counter stools because their seats are too hard. Instead, she sits at the banquette by the window, which, unlike the one in the back door, is clean. She watches Alma move steadily around the kitchen. She's an untroubled soul, though Angie is certain she's had her share. She never married. Her only sibling, a sister, doesn't like her much. Sometimes she hears from her niece in Iowa. No cards arrive on her birthday or at Christmas. She worked for Chip while his first wife was alive, and their three boys ran wild around the place. She would have been about Angie's age then. Angie tries to imagine being in her late sixties. What will she have to look back on?

"I hear you've got a beau," Alma says, putting a thick sandwich of salami and cheese on rye in front of her. She's been thoughtful enough to add a juicy pickle, which Angie devours first.

"Yeah."

"What's he do?"

"Tends bar. Plays guitar."

"Gets stuck in tar?"

"Huh?"

"You were on a roll there."

Alma joins her. She huffs as she lowers herself onto the seat. She's built like a soup can, and the space between the table and her stomach is tight. They eat without talking for a few minutes. Angie polishes off her sandwich; Alma eats slowly.

Angie tells her about Matt's sister. Then she talks about the drug bust at the bar and how the server who got caught dealing keeps calling Matt.

"Why?" Alma asks.

"He says just to talk."

"They good friends?"

"I didn't think so. I mean, I don't know if they are or aren't. I assumed they aren't."

"Because you figure a guy that good-looking doesn't have women friends, only girlfriends."

"Something like that. Wait, who said Matt was good-looking?"

"Isn't he?"

"Yes, very."

110

"Well, there you go."

Alma leans back and burps softly. Angie hopes she'll say something reassuring about Sharon and Matt, that she has nothing to worry about, that he's just trying to be nice.

"I had a boyfriend once that really did have a girl who was a friend," Alma said.

"Really?"

"It was a long time ago."

"Go on."

Alma says well, this was back in the sixties when just about everything changed between men and women. For one thing, women were no longer "good girls" or "bad girls." Angie must know what she's talking about, she's probably seen the old movie, *Where The Boys Are?* Where these college girls go to Florida for spring break and meet up with a bunch of guys there for the same reason, and what's her-name, Paula Prentiss, ends up on the beach at night with her particular young man and he asks her if she's a good girl. Meaning, is she going to sleep with him? And she says no, she's not.

Anyhow, Alma was about 18 and her fellow was 19, and they were just crazy about each other. Thank god for the pill, that's all she could say. She was convinced that they were going to move into together, though secretly she wanted to get married. She wasn't supposed to think like that. Marriage was a trap, so everyone said. There was this girl the boyfriend knew from school. They grew up together, hung out, shared secrets, offered advice on all sorts of things like what clothes to wear, what books to read, who they should be friends with, who they should avoid. The fact was, this girl knew a lot more about him than Alma did, and it just didn't sit right. She told herself it was normal, given how much time they'd spent together, but the plain truth was that Alma was jealous, and a jealous woman doesn't think straight. She assumed they were hiding something from her, that they were in love.

She confronted the boyfriend, who said, "If we *were* in love, why would we bother hiding it?" Alma backed down, but she never stopped thinking about it, even after she came to see that there really was nothing romantic between them. The real trouble, she realized, is that she was pretty sure the boyfriend talked to the friend about her, and that put her at a disadvantage.

"But what if he talked about you to a guy he was friends with? Would that have bothered you?" Angie asked.

"No. Guys talking to each other about girls is normal. A guy talking to one girl about another girl isn't."

Angie has to wonder if Matt talks to Sharon about *her*. But, why would he? What turn would a conversation have to take for her to become the subject of it?

Alma takes their plates and puts them in the sink. She stands with her hands on her hips, gazing out the window behind Angie. Lavinia's heels can be heard coming closer. She enters the kitchen, followed by the heady aroma of expensive perfume. She wears a jacket and a matching skirt. Her hair is up.

"What are you doing out of bed?" she asks Angie.

"I'm fine. I took a day off."

Lavinia marches over and puts her hand on her forehead.

"Hmm," she says.

"You on your way?" Alma asks her.

"Just about."

"Where are you going?" Angie asks.

"Taking your father to lunch."

"Wait, I was supposed to be there."

"I'll handle this round. You can take the next one."

Angie is actually relieved. She doesn't feel like dealing with her father today.

"Did your invitation surprise him?" Alma asks.

"Who knows? Man's got a good poker face. Or voice, in this case."

"Mind the ice in those stilts."

"I'll be fine."

Lavinia takes a fur coat out of the hall closet and slips into it. Women in Dunston don't wear fur, even wealthy ones. Dunston is a laid-back college town. It's just like her mother not to care.

When she's gone Alma announces that she's going to make bread. She asks if Angie wants to help her.

"Sure."

Alma tells Angie where to find a large bowl. The mixer is already on the counter. Alma measures warm water and pours it into the bowl, tears open a couple of packets of yeast, begins mixing the water and yeast on low speed and adds in three cups of flour. Angie watches. When the dough has formed a ball, Alma turns off the mixer and lifts the arm so she can pluck if off the attachment. She tells Angie to sprinkle some flour from the canister right there on the quartz countertop. As Angie jiggles the scoop gently in a back and forth motion, the falling flour is like snow. Alma plops the dough down and pats it.

"You want to knead it?" she asks Angie.

"How?"

"Use the heels of your hands. Here."

Alma shows her how to dig in and stretch the dough. Angie tries. She expects the dough to feel gross on her skin, but it doesn't. It feels wonderful, almost as if it's alive. Alma tells her to turn it and knead from the bottom edge. The dough yields and lengthens, as if it wants to please her. She keeps kneading and turning until Alma tells her to stop. It's time to put the dough back in the bowl and cover it so it can rise.

"Then what?" Angie asks.

"We wait for about an hour and a half."

"Oh, man!"

"I didn't write the rules."

Alma covers the bowl with plastic wrap and washes her hands. Then Angie washes hers. As Zen as kneading the dough was, she's not about to kill that kind of time just hanging around waiting for step two.

She calls Matt. He says she woke him up, but that it's okay. She asks when he goes on shift, and he says not till the late afternoon. Does he want to hang out until then?

"Aren't you at work?"

"Day off."

"Cool."

He suggests they go skiing. Cross-country, not downhill. He skis? He learned a couple of years ago. She doesn't have skis. He has a pair he thinks might be her size. She wonders why. Maybe they were the former girlfriend's. Angie's never been on a pair of skis in her life and tells him so.

"You'll pick it up in no time," he says.

"What should I wear?"

"Something warm and comfortable. You got any stretch pants? Maybe a pair of long underwear you can put on under them?"

"I'll figure something out."

Angie returns home and digs through her wardrobe. She finds a pair of dress slacks that have a spandex waist. As to the long underwear, she substitutes a pair of heavy tights. She wears a turtleneck top under a lightweight pull-over sweater. Over that she wears a quilted jacket that makes her look like the Michelin Man. Her hair is shoulder length and trying to tie it up is impossible. She stuffs it under the rim of her funky wool cap, but that makes her head look lopsided and deformed. She wishes she were the kind of woman who looks good in anything, like her mother.

Matt has several pairs of ski boots that Angie tries on. One fits, but only with the extra pair of socks that he lends her. He looks her over from head to toe and laughs. Then he kisses her. He straps the skis to the rack on top of his car and they set off for a trail system about six miles outside of town. He asks her for an update on her father. Angie says her mother took him to lunch.

"So, they still see each other?" he asks.

"Not really. They talk on the phone now and then."

There are only a handful of cars in the lot because it's a weekday. They park, unload the skis, and Matt buckles her into hers. She instantly feels off-balance and says there's no way this is going to work.

He's patient. He tells her to pivot forward and back and to get used to the feel of the poles in her hand. He puts on his own skis and shows her a basic stride forward.

"Push with your toes, like this," he says, gliding a few feet away. She tries and finds the effort overwhelming. She's already sweating. He comes back and positions himself right next to her and says, "Left, right, left, right. See?"

She makes minimal progress.

"I get it. It's a rhythm, you know, just like . ." She looks at him and blushes. He throws his head back and laughs.

"You have a dirty mind," he says.

"Oh, and you didn't think of that, I suppose."

He hands her a pair of goggles from the pocket of his jacket. The lenses are yellow, and they're secured with an elastic band that wraps around the back of her head. He has a pair for himself, too. His eyes look strange as he peers at her through them, like himself, but not.

She lurches forward, determined to gain ground. The trail ascends slightly through some trees, and there the effort almost does her in. She uses an elliptical at the gym, so why is this so hard?

Matt's a few feet ahead of her, moving gracefully, sharing encouraging words as they go.

"Just keep at it, it'll get easier," he says.

It doesn't, but at least the trail levels out.

They continue, single file. The recent snow is soft and powdery. The shadows cast by the trees are purplish-blue. The air stings her nose as she inhales; her breath plumes as she chugs ahead.

She concentrates on her stride, finds it, loses it, then finds it again. Her insulated mittens are too big and gripping the pole handles is a challenge. For all the discomfort and frustration, she finds that concentrating on her body and how it moves frees her. She's not anxious, irritated, or frustrated, but calm, centered, free of the confines of her daily life. This must be what people love about the outdoors. She felt this sometimes as a girl, sledding down a hill, loving the rush of wind, the rising speed, not knowing just where the sled would come to rest.

As she becomes more certain of her pace, she lifts her head. Matt's not there. She can't see him up ahead, either, though her view of the trail is clear for a long way. She stops, calls his name, and listens. All she hears is the wind as it sends down flurries of snow from the tree branches.

She goes on, skiing harder. A couple comes towards her and she stops them to ask if they've seen anyone up ahead. They're not sure, they weren't really paying attention. They resume, at a rapid, expert pace.

The further along the trail she goes, the madder she gets. She yanks off a mitten, takes her phone from her pocket, and calls Matt's number. It goes right to voice mail. She thinks she remembers him putting his phone in the glove compartment of his car. She puts the phone back and moves on. After what feels like a long time, she comes to a clearing with a spectacular view of the valley below, and there is Matt, taking it all in.

"Hey!" she yells. His head turns, his smile is instant. He glides towards her and comes to a well-controlled stop.

"Where the hell were you?" she asks.

"I just went ahead a little."

"I couldn't even see you."

"Yeah, I ski fast when I get going."

"Well, I don't."

"I was just having fun."

"At my expense."

"How, at your expense?"

She says she doesn't know how to ski, this is her first time, and what if she'd fallen down and couldn't get back up?

"You're stronger than you think," he says.

"That's not the point! You put a beginner on a pair of skis, then take off and leave her to fend for herself."

Her voice is loud, and when she stops talking, the silence sounds even louder.

"You're right, I'm sorry," he says.

Something inside her tilts. She wants to right it and can't. In no time she's crying, her shoulders bobbing up and down.

Her face is wet and cold. Matt has his arms around her which warms her up but doesn't slow the sobs. First the breakdown in Nancy's office, then the trickle in front of her mother, and now this. She hasn't cried so much since . . . Blake Rawls dumped her. Why is she so fragile?

"Hey, it's okay," Matt says.

"Oh, God. I'm sorry."

"Let's get you home." Matt helps her turn around on the trail, puts her in the lead, and matches her ridiculously slow pace. Having to focus again on keeping herself in motion and upright soothes her, though she feels deeply ashamed of losing control. When they reach the car Matt helps her out of her skis, then removes his. Next, they take off their ski boots and get into their regular ones. He unlocks the door so she can sit while he gets the skis back on the rack. He offers to turn the engine so she can have heat. She says she's fine.

They drive in silence. Then Matt asks, "What's it all about, anyway?"

"I thought you wouldn't come back."

"But I would have if you hadn't found me."

They're on the outskirts of Dunston now. The sky to the north has gone from blue to opaque gray, suggesting a change in the weather.

They pull into the parking lot of his apartment complex. A minute later they're inside. Matt hangs their jackets in the small closet by the front door. She helps herself to the couch. Matt joins her. He puts his arm around her.

"Did someone leave you to fend for yourself when you were young?" he asks.

"My mother, but only for a while. She came back, packed us all up, and took us away."

"Anyone else? A man? You never talk about your past relationships."

She tells him about Blake, then about Brett, then lastly about Jerry, qualifying the tale by saying that she was in love with Blake, sometimes in love with Brett, and never in love with Jerry.

"So, your heart got harder each time," Matt says.

"Not so hard I can't love."

"I hope not."

He looks like he's going to lean in and kiss her. Angie sits perfectly still, and the moment passes.

"I can see why you're leery of guys, with that track record," Matt says. A spark of anger flares within her, but she quenches it with reason. He's just trying to figure things out, to figure *her* out. And he's more or less correct.

"I guess we bring into each new relationship all the baggage from the ones before," she says.

"For sure."

She stretches her legs. Her thigh muscles protest. She's going to be sore tomorrow. She thinks longingly of the deep soaking tub she saved up for last year and was finally able to have installed. She hasn't used it in months.

"What about you? Any exes out there still haunting you?" Angie asks.

"One."

"Go on."

He says her name is Celine, and they were together for a couple of years. At the end of the day, she wasn't a happy person, wasn't happy with herself. She had an eating disorder. She was way too thin. She worked with a therapist, and even though she stopped losing weight, she had trouble being in a relationship. She needed so much personal space that Matt felt he was only ever visiting, not truly with her. It was hard to reach her, and one day he gave up trying. Rather than being devastated, she seemed relieved.

Angie wonders if this is the same woman Sam described to her the other night. Can someone go from being anorexic to being overweight?

"So, what are *you* leery of?" she asks, keeping a light, pleasant tone as if she's merely curious.

"I don't know. Being shut out, I suppose."

"I promise not to do that."

"I know."

"How can you know?"

"Well, you're pretty direct. You don't seem like you're hiding a lot of stuff."

Angie is taken aback. She thinks of herself as mysterious, hard to read. Then she sees that what Matt's observed is emotional honesty in the form of grief and irritation that often borders on anger.

"Okay, well to be direct, I need to ask you a question," she says.

"Shoot."

"Did you and Sharon have a romantic relationship?"

"You're asking if I have more than friendly feelings for her."

"Yes.

Matt breathes slowly, almost deliberately. Angie tenses. She wishes she'd said nothing, yet knows the matter has to be raised sooner or later, and she far prefers that she be the one to raise it.

"I thought I did, but no," Matt says.

"When did you think you did?"

"Before I met you, and a little afterward."

"So, you developed feelings for me while you thought you might have them for her."

"Something like that."

"I see."

"You're not going to get mad at me again, are you? Because I can only take getting yelled at once a day."

Angie can't tell if he's being funny or not. She gives him the benefit of the doubt.

"No, I'm not going to get mad."

"Good."

He says he knew Sharon from the last place he worked, a bar on campus where she liked to go. She usually came in alone, sometimes with friends, hardly ever with just a guy. They got talking one night and he said he was thinking of looking for a new gig, and she suggested he come down to The Watering Hole and talk to Gus.

After he started there, they hung out sometimes after work, but it was always at the bar, after their shifts, never anywhere else. He didn't know she was dealing then, of course. He didn't find out about that until she got arrested. He never saw her selling drugs, in fact, he said so when the cops interviewed him. He doesn't know how she pulled it off, and he's never asked. The truth is, he just doesn't want to know.

Angie wonders if the edge in his voice means he lost respect for her then. If that's true, why does he still talk to her so much on the phone?

She asks him.

"Well, as I say, she's pretty freaked out," he says.

"Yeah, but why does she lean on you? Isn't there anyone else?"

"I don't know."

"Maybe you feel guilty."

"Why would I feel guilty?"

"Because she thought you guys were tight in a way you weren't, and you feel bad for letting her think something that wasn't true."

Matt looks at her. She can tell she caught him off guard.

"She said she was in love with me," he said.

"When?"

"I don't know. After we got to be friends."

"Does she still say it?"

"Yes."

"And what do you say?"

"That I don't feel the same."

And yet, Sharon persists. She may have gotten caught with her coke, but she's never struck Angie as stupid, certainly not as a girl with stars in her eyes.

"You slept together," Angie says.

"Yeah."

"More than once?"

"Yeah."

"The last time being?"

"A week before I met you."

Does she believe him? She *wants* to. That's an improvement. She'll have to tell Nancy.

"Thank you for being so honest with me," she says.

"I'm an honest guy."

She kisses him. He responds. It's all of two minutes until they're in his room, toppling into bed.

chapter eleven

Lynn's MP3 file is giving Angie trouble. First, it won't download. Then there's no sound. Angie sees that the volume on her desktop is turned all the way down. It's Monday, she's cleared out a half-hour to listen to what Lynn curated. Her email that morning thanks Angie so much for making time for her, and she hopes they'll have a chance to get together again soon. Angie notes Lynn's enthusiasm and wishes she had a fraction of it.

First up is Mr. Jenkins. Lynn's editing isn't perfect. Her voice says, "Oops, hit the wrong button again, hang on, okay, here we go …" Then when Mr. Jenkins begins, he says, "You want me to talk into that? What is that, a phone?"

Then he's all business. He states his name, where he was born (Dayton, Ohio) and the year (1940). He describes his education, a love of scientific inquiry, falling in love with a girl named Bridgette, then one named Hannah, and after her a Sarah-Jane, whom he married. Sarah-Jane couldn't have children. They didn't want to adopt. That was your only option back then, not like today, when they give you the shots or whatever to make the baby take. He got a job teaching at Ohio Wesleyan in 1961; Sarah-Jane was a housewife, and they had a lot of cats, despite the fact that he was allergic to them. Sarah-Jane was the kind of woman worth making sacrifices for.

Mr. Jenkins pauses and asks Lynn for some water. With a dry chuckle, he tells her to mix it with bourbon. He doesn't need ice. Never took it on the rocks. Lynn gets him the water and tells him she'd love a bourbon and branch, too, if she had any on her. Humoring a resident, joining them in their momentary flight of fancy, is a gift. Angie used to have it. Does she still?

Angie hears Mr. Jenkins put the plastic cup on the table by his wheelchair. He says nothing for a long time. Lynn clears her throat. After another long pause, during which Angie imagines Mr. Jenkins forgets what he was saying, stares at his hands, plucks the fibers on the blanket that rests in his lap, or leers at Lynn, he speaks.

His only sister, Judith, didn't like Sarah-Jane. That was the plain truth, the long and short of it. Judith was very particular about people. He hopes Lynn understands what he means is, she was a snob. Sarah-Jane was an extraordinary person living an ordinary life if that makes sense, but all Judith could see was Sarah-Jane's lopsided pineapple upside-down cake, her bargain-basement shoes, and the wallpaper she chose for the dining room, with milkmaids in white bonnets. Judith was only exposed to these things once a year when she and her husband Marvin came out from California. Marvin worked for a defense contractor there. Made a bundle. Judith was above herself long before she had Marvin's money to spend; she was in the stratosphere afterward.

Sarah-Jane knew Judith looked down on her. She couldn't miss it with a ten-foot pole. She tried to jolly her out of it, she was a good sport that way, but Judith was a sourpuss. Sarah-Jane didn't really care about the cake, her silly shoes, or her loud wallpaper all that much. Her pride was in her garden. Raised dahlias, roses, and the most beautiful lilies you ever saw. Judith knew these flowers were first-rate, so what did she do? She asked Sarah-Jane if she were going to bulldoze them under and put in a swimming pool. Judith had had too much dessert wine that evening. Marvin kept nudging her under the table every time she lifted her glass. Judith called from the airport the next day to say she was sorry and when he offered to put Sarah-Jane on so she could tell her herself, she said she had to go. He knew for a fact that her plane didn't leave for a good hour after that. She just chickened out.

Mr. Jenkins cut Judith off after that. He wrote to her and said her cruelty was unforgivable. Judith protested. They were blood. That's what mattered. Mr. Jenkins held firm. It was a matter of principle.

In time, he saw he'd done it for himself more than for Sarah-Jane because Sarah-Jane got over the insult soon enough. Maybe he was looking for a reason to push Judith out. They'd never really gotten along all that well. She'd been their mother's favorite, maybe that's what ate at him.

Lynn interrupts.

"How long has it been since you were in touch with your sister?" she asks.

Again a long, painful pause.

"Fifty-five years. I don't even know if she's still alive."

Angie expects Lynn to suggest that he can find out if he wants to, or that someone could look into the matter for him, but she wisely keeps quiet. She doesn't want to turn his thoughts in a new direction. It's better if he can ease himself out of what he led himself into.

"For a long time, I was sure I'd done the right thing," Mr. Jenkins says. "But then I'd see her everywhere—walking on a sidewalk, standing in line at the bank, even driving past. Of course, it was never her, just someone who looked like her, or like what I figured she would look like. And I saw her kids—did I say she and Marvin had kids? You're wondering how I knew that, if I wasn't in touch, right? Well, Marvin made sure I got news now and then. I guess it bothered him that we didn't have anything to do with each other, I don't know. Maybe he was just trying to rub my nose in how well they'd done without me in their lives. I never really got a good read on him."

Of course, since no pictures ever came, all he did was imagine these children. He assumed the girls had Judith's dark hair; the boys had Marvin's height. Years would pass, and then he'd see a little boy

125

or girl and be sure he was looking at a niece or nephew. He knew he couldn't be when he calculated how much time had actually gone by.

There's nothing after that, not even a closing comment from Lynn. Angie closes the file. She can't listen to the rest of it right now. She writes an email to Lynn saying she did an amazing job, to please type everything up, and send the hard copy to Sherry, with an added remark that Sherry is old school and would rather read from a piece of paper than from a screen.

Just as Angie is leaving for lunch, Lavinia calls with an update on her lunch with Potter. Angie feels a stab of guilt for not checking back on that situation, herself. She knows she resisted doing so because she doesn't want to offer herself as any sort of caretaker or custodian at the moment. Confronting her reluctance only makes her feel worse because the person in question is her beloved father, after all.

They went to Madeleine's, a lovely French restaurant Lavinia is particularly fond of. Potter seemed fine, happy that she called, glad to get out of the house. When Lavinia asked how Mary Beth was, his answer was a shrug.

She let him get through two drinks before she got to the point. To her surprise, he didn't evade or make light of the matter. He said he'd gotten sloppy again and was going to rein in the consumption soon.

"Sounds like another false promise," Angie says.

"Your father's promises are never false. They're just seldom kept."

"How did he seem overall?"

Lavinia pauses.

"Handsome and charming as ever," she says. "He said things were pretty sour between him and Mary Beth and that he hoped that wouldn't keep me from hiring her to remodel this dump. My word, not his. I didn't tell him I only called her because I had a sense that things weren't all beer and skittles with them. No point in flattering the old fool more than need be."

Lavinia pauses again.

"Mom?"

"I told him to hightail it out of there."

"Wait, you told him to leave her?"

"I did."

What else did she expect? Her mother is as subtle as a brick.

As Lavinia talks on, this time about the details of the meal itself, including the salad dressing and what kind of music was on the sound system, a notification pops up on Angie's computer screen from Facebook Messenger. It's from Lynn. She's really happy Angie likes her report. There's only one thing. She's still thinking about Lillian.

It's hard to think of her keeping that secret for so many years, don't you think?

Angie answers, *Yes, it really is.*

A minute later, *Is there anything you can do?*

I'm not sure what you mean.

Like counsel her or help her. I don't know. I'm babbling.

Angie promises to talk to Sherry and work out a plan.

Lynn closes with, *Let's get together for a drink or something. You're a hoot!*

A hoot? That's a new one.

"So, I asked him flat out if he was still in love with her," Lavinia says.

"Mom, listen, I need to get going. Can I call you later?"

"Well, sure, if you don't want to hear what he said."

"What did he say?"

"That he never was."

This confirms what Lavinia suggested the other night. Angie understands about marriages of convenience. Her mother's liaison with Chip was a practical endeavor, not an affair of the heart.

What about her and Matt? Is she just using him for sex? It occurs to her that she hasn't really assessed her feelings for him. Something keeps getting in the way. Fear, of course. But there's another thing she can't identify.

Maybe she's just too used to being alone. Set in her ways, Alma would say. Everyone expects you to couple up, live together, complete each other, but what if somehow, she's made *less* by being with someone? That there are parts of herself she has to close off, lest she offend or intimidate or damage? Is there a difference between that and just having a normal filter on normal emotions?

"Does marriage change you?" Angie asks.

"What?"

"I'm sorry. That was a weird question."

"It was. But yes, if you want your marriage to work, you have to rise up to meet it." Then Lavinia says *she* has to go and will be in touch later.

The dropping temperature outside steers Angie towards the cafeteria, but then the idea becomes too much. Even though the meatloaf is outstanding, she needs fresh air on her face. She sprints across the lot to her car. The maintenance crew neglected to salt a patch of ice and down she goes, right on her butt. Her tailbone wails. She broke it once, as a kid, flying off a sled badly piloted by Timothy. The weeks it took to heal present themselves now in terms of the bedroom pleasures she may have to forgo. She rolls over on to her knees, grabs the door handle, and pulls herself up. She rubs her backside and determines that the bone is intact, just bruised.

128

Later, as she stands in line at the deli, waiting for her roast beef on rye, her phone rings. It's Foster. Potter called him earlier that morning, asking if they could do lunch.

"So?" Angie asks. A muscle in her lower back feels wrenched from the fall.

"He didn't sound good."

"Uh, oh."

"I told him to come over. He's taking a nap."

"You need me over there?"

"Only if you can get away."

Sherry's in meetings all day up in Syracuse. Angie asks Foster if he's got food in the house since Potter will need to eat something hearty when he wakes up. Foster says he made soup the day before. Angie asks what kind.

"Chicken noodle," he says.

"From scratch?"

"Of course."

Does he want her to pick up anything?

"A six-pack of beer."

"That's the last thing he needs."

"I meant for me."

Angie knows Foster doesn't drink. She appreciates his black humor.

She eats while she drives, spilling crumbs and lettuce in her lap. Snow falls, and she can tell by its strength another five or six inches will be on the ground by dinnertime. Maybe she should buy a pair of cross-country skis and practice so the next time she and Matt hit the trails she'll be ready. Or they could try snowshoeing, but that sounds like even more work than skiing.

This is Angie's first visit to the home Foster is housesitting. It's a lovely place, with built-in bookcases, a stone fireplace, lead glass windows on either side, refinished wood floors, and beautiful modern furniture built low with sleek lines. On the red sofa Potter lies with one arm thrown over his head. Foster has put a blanket over him and removed his shoes. Angie smells liquor as she passes. They go into the kitchen, which is as nice as the living room. Foster must enjoy staying there. He's wearing sweatpants and a sweatshirt that can't conceal how thin he really is. He eats a lot and always has, and never seems to gain a pound. Mad Max sits on a wide windowsill, watching the snow. There's a heating vent just below, which explains his fondness for that particular spot. Angie realizes she doesn't smell cat pee. Foster's done a good job getting Mad Max to use a litter box.

He takes Angie's coat and puts it in the closet behind the kitchen. On the stove is a large ceramic pot. He turns on the fire below it. His movements are calm, confident, despite their father's drunken presence. Foster, like Angie, like all of them, is a veteran of his lapses.

Foster got the story about Mary Beth from Timothy and thinks Potter should confront her directly.

"You mean ask her if she's having an affair?" Angie asks.

"Ask her what she plans to do about Dad. He's her responsibility." Foster puts on a fancy striped apron and slices a good-looking loaf of French bread.

Angie looks probingly at Foster. He looks at her just as intently, then sighs and shakes his head. He means that he can't have Potter move in with him there, in the professor's house. It's too risky, with all their nice things around. They both know Timothy and Sam don't have the room for him. If Angie weren't involved with Matt, it might be okay to give him her second bedroom. But her privacy is crucial to her now. She feels bad for closing her door to him.

"I'm 34 years old, for God's sake," she says. Foster glances her way but doesn't ask her to clarify that statement. She hopes he understands.

He puts the plate of sliced bread on the table in front of Angie, along with a second smaller plate into which he's drizzled olive oil and balsamic vinegar. Though she's full from lunch, Angie helps herself, which makes another nagging voice speak up in her head. She takes a single bite of bread and has no more.

"Mom took him to lunch, I hear," Foster says.

"Yeah."

"Brave woman."

"She wants to help."

At this, Foster's expression turns grim. He's still angry at their mother for leaving their father all those years ago. The times he and Angie have discussed this, she asked what exactly he expected their mother to do. He never had a good answer. He just wishes the situation never came up, the situation they're stuck with again now—Potter's love of alcohol.

A soft moan comes from the living room, followed by a series of dry coughs. Angie and Foster stay put. A moment later, Potter appears, smoothing down his hair and tucking in his striped button-down shirt. His gait is off from the liquor. Angie is glad he walked over, rather than getting behind the wheel. It's good he knows when driving is a bad idea. A drinking problem must be like having migraines, or any condition that flares up from time to time, she thinks. You learn how to give it space.

His face lights up when he sees Angie. His arms open in greeting.

"Hey, there!" he says.

"Hey, Dad."

"You joining us for lunch?"

"Ate already."

"Ah."

Potter helps himself to a chair. He peers out at the snow. "Really coming down," he says.

Foster stands behind him, a hand on Potter's shoulder, and asks if he's hungry.

"Sure! Smells good in here."

He and Foster eat. The conversation is all about the holidays and what everyone wants to see under the tree. Angie describes the cross-country skiing fiasco. Foster laughs at the thought of her chugging up a trail. He's not making fun of her, just reveling in the unlikeliness of it.

"I knew that guy would be good for you," Potter says.

Mad Max is now under the table, staring up at Potter with love.

"Dad, listen, we're all worried about you," Angie says.

Potter nods solemnly. He sighs and leans back.

"I know, I know, things have been a little rough lately," he says.

"You're drinking like a fish," Foster says. Angie's caught off guard. Foster's not usually so blunt.

"Only had a couple so far today," Potter says.

"It's one o'clock in the afternoon," Foster says.

"Yeah, well, I got troubles, you know?"

"Mary Beth," Angie says.

"And that jackass she's . . . consorting with."

"Have you talked to her?" Angie asks.

"About a million times."

"And?"

"And nothing. She denies everything."

"But you know it's true."

"Yeah."

"How?"

Once again Potter lifts his hand to smooth down his hair.

The guy came to see him at Mary Beth's design studio. They know where it is, right? Angie and Foster shake their heads though they've both heard Mary Beth speak of it more than once.

Anyway, Potter went to school with the guy, Jason Keller. He was a jerk then and he's a jerk now, and not just because he's doing his wife. Jason's one of those guys who thinks he owns the whole damn world. Entitled, you know? Head the size of Christmas ham and a ping-pong ball for a brain. He's a snappy dresser, okay, Potter can give him that. And he's a great realtor if you're into great realtors, which apparently Mary Beth is. She no doubt sees him as a business opportunity. He sells the houses, she remodels them. Or, maybe they'll get into flipping. He'll buy them, she'll fix them, then he'll unload them on some poor sucker for a lot more than they're worth.

"Why did he come to see you?" Angie asks.

Oh, that. Well, he wanted to do the right thing, you know, since he's such a standup guy. He knows it's hard to hear that his wife has fallen for someone else, but that's the long and short of it. He just hopes there are no hard feelings. Mary Beth's a great gal—yeah, he used that word —and he hopes Potter just wants the best for her.

"What did you do?" Foster asks.

"I told him to get the hell out."

"When did all this happen?" Angie asks.

"Oh, I don't know. A few weeks ago, at least."

"You mean before I came to dinner?"

"Yup."

"But why the act?"

133

"What act?"

"You guys behaving like nothing's wrong."

"Because I told her she was going to mind her damn Ps and Qs in front of my daughter."

Angie's heart swells with love.

"Look, I'm sorry I showed up here a little the worse for wear," Potter says. "It's just been a tough time, and I haven't been as disciplined as I should be. Your mother had other words for my . . . *foibles*, needless to say. Bless her." He smiles at some memory, whether it was something that happened long ago or just the other day, Angie has no way of knowing.

"You need to stop drinking so much," Foster says. He clears the table. The cat follows him into the kitchen. Foster tells it no, it's not getting a snack now.

Potter nods. "I will. As soon as this thing with Mary Beth gets sorted out."

Angie asks him what he means by sorted out. He says resolved, put in the past, so they can move forward.

"You're saying this is a fling, and she'll get over it?" Foster asks.

"Well, no. I don't think she'll get over it."

"Are you saying you guys are going to split up?" Angie asks.

"That's about the gist of it."

Angie says he needs to keep a clear head in the weeks and months ahead. Now is not the time to jump down a bottle of bourbon. He has plans to make, a life to rebuild, all sorts of things he's going to have to handle on his own now.

Foster makes coffee, and the kitchen fills with a rich, comforting smell. Potter uses the bathroom; Angie checks her phone; Foster puts Mad Max back on the windowsill and rubs his head, making him purr madly.

Potter emerges. He looks calmer, more in control of himself.

"Don't worry about me," Potter says, taking his seat. "I won't be on my own."

"What do you mean?" Angie asks.

Potter looks surprised. "Didn't your mother tell you? I'm moving in with her and Alma."

"Oh my god."

"Oh my god, what? She offered. It's not like she doesn't have room for me."

Foster and Angie look at each other. She hopes he won't say anything.

"Yeah, it's a big house for sure. And Alma's a good cook. You'll like that," she says.

"Yeah."

They all look out the window then and remark on the snow. It's falling harder by the minute.

chapter twelve

The Commons shine with Christmas decorations. The sky is the color of chrome, the sidewalks are littered with salt crunching underfoot. Matt wants to find his mother a gift and asked Angie if she can help.

Christmas is three weeks away and everything is crowded. Plus, it's Saturday. Matt's got the whole day off. They're having dinner at Angie's later. She's laid in a chicken she's going to roast, potatoes to mash, and a couple of boxes of frozen creamed spinach. She wonders about picking up a small cake for dessert, then thinks of the calories already in her menu and decides against it.

They talk about Potter moving in with Lavinia. Matt says it's the craziest thing he's ever heard. His own parents divorced when he was 12. Their relationship turned bitter just before then and never recovered. Both his mother and father cite his sister's drug problem as evidence of the other's parental failings. It makes him sad sometimes to think of them so at odds when they once must have been deeply in love.

Angie says it's too bad when people get on the wrong side of each other after being aligned. What she doesn't say is that it astonishes her that people ever get along well enough to make any sort of lasting commitment in the first place.

"What about this?" Matt asks and pushes a lavender sachet towards her. They're in a shop that sells scented candles, specialty soaps, and all sorts of things that make Angie's nose itch.

"Does she like girlie things like that?" Angie asks.

"No." Matt puts the sachet back.

They move on to a display of hand-carved boxes, some inlaid with mother-of-pearl. One has small turquoise stones on the lid. He picks it up. The interior is lined with blue velvet. He looks at Angie and says, "I don't know why, but this reminds me of you."

"Me?"

"Yeah. You're so pretty on the outside, and so soft on the inside."

"Oh, stop."

They wander around the store some more. Angie senses Matt's restlessness. She asks him to tell her about his mother, what she likes, what she doesn't like, what kinds of things she has in her home, anything she's particularly fond of.

Matt pauses, and a look of fond whimsy fills his eyes.

The woman has no taste, he says, which should make it easy to buy for her, but the problem is there are just some things he can't stoop to, like adding to her collection of ceramic owls. They're all over the place. She's collected them forever.

Angie says the owl is a symbol of wisdom, and that's a charming idea, right?

Matt says his mother is definitely wise. That's why she was such a good teacher.

"What does she teach?"

"English, before she retired."

"I didn't know that."

"Because I just told you." He pinches her playfully on the arm. Angie takes his hand and kisses it. He puts his arm around her as they continue their random tour.

He says his mother's boyfriend hates the owls. He's into Japanese bonsai trees. They argue about where the trees should go since so much space is taken up with the owls.

"They live together?" Angie asks.

"Yeah. For years."

a winter night

Suddenly Angie feels much less sorry for the mother, whom she pictured as sadly divorced, living alone, grieving the plight of her addicted daughter, wishing her only son were closer. It occurs to her with a jolt that one day she'll probably meet her. It will be important to Matt that she like Angie, and that Angie like her. Angie knows she's a good faker and can be warm and pleasant with anyone for a limited time. Maybe the mother's the same way.

Why does she assume his mother won't like her? What crazy clutch of insecurity is that?

Almost an hour and four stores later, they find a small carved owl with red stones for eyes. They laugh at how awful it is and agree that Matt's mother will no doubt adore it.

"What's her name?" Angie asks.

"Mom? Clair."

"Pretty."

"Suits her. She's a good-looking woman."

"Now I know where you get it from."

"I look like my dad."

"Handsome devil, eh?"

Matt's brow furrows, but only for a moment. Clearly, she said the wrong thing.

They walk arm in arm out of the Commons and into the adjoining neighborhood where they parked. Wreaths are on doors; lights are strung on fences and porches. One house's bare maple is decorated with small blue bulbs that flash on and off. All this cheer, Angie thinks. All this hope. For what? Happiness? Joy? Just getting through to New Year's?

Matt's phone rings and he stops to answer it. His face stills.

"Well, that's good, right?" he says. Angie leans closer, trying to hear the caller and can't.

"Look, I'm in the middle of something, so I'll catch you later, okay?" he says. "Yeah, okay, love ya." He hangs up.

"Who was that?" Angie asks.

"Sharon. She's been assigned a public defender. About time. She was getting jerked around."

They walk on, not touching. Angie's temples throb, and her hands sweat inside her leather gloves. She loosens her wool scarf. The air feels like it's about eighty degrees. They stop at a light. The building on the corner is a converted Victorian mansion housing professional offices. As a little girl, Angie thought it would grand it would be to live there, with her bedroom in the cupola facing the street, where she could sit and watch the world pass, day by day, and not have to be a part of it unless she wanted to. Sometimes she imagined her family living there, too, all of them happy, having the usual frictions that passed quickly with smiles and kisses. In her child's mind, her father was a great thinker who immersed himself in books. His library was a quiet, wonderful place. He let her come in whenever she wanted and sit with her own slim volume of poetry while he absorbed the battles of the ancient world; the fall of empires; the rise of the industrial revolution. Only she was allowed, no one else. The light turns green, they pass the building, and Angie returns to winter. She feels cold all the way down to her toes.

"Why did you say that?" she asks.

"Say what?"

"'Love ya.'"

"Because she said it to me."

Angie's pace slows imperceptibly at first, then more, until Matt is a stride ahead of her. He's half a block up when he realizes she's stopped. His expression is one of genuine surprise. The smile is tentative. The hands are out of the pockets now, and his head, which had been bent against the cold lifts as if to get a better view of her.

139

"You love her?" Angie asks.

"No, of course not."

"You said you did."

"No, I didn't."

"You said, 'love ya.' How is that not saying you love her?"

Matt closes the distance between them. He puts his hands on her shoulders. "It's just something you say, that's all."

A man with a newspaper under his arm passes them on the sidewalk. A minute later a woman carrying two grocery bags goes by from the opposite direction. A dog barks from inside a house. A few blocks away, a car alarm sounds annoyingly and then is silenced.

Matt removes his hands. "What do you want from me?"

Angie focuses on his words and the tone of his voice. She detects no pleading, no attempt to make things right, only a heaviness, fatigue.

"Do you love her, yes or no?" Angie stares at the slate sidewalk.

"Yes. But as a friend only."

"A friend you slept with."

"That's in the past."

"How can you ever really be just a friend with someone with you slept with?"

"I don't know. But that's how it is with me and Sharon. You've got to believe me."

Angie looks him in the eye. She sees herself reflected there. Something goes out of her like a slow leak that picks up speed, emptying her in seconds.

"I don't have to do anything, Matt," she says.

"What's that supposed to mean?"

"It means I don't want to see you again until you figure out where your heart is."

140

"I know where my heart is."

She shakes her head. The stream reverses course now, flowing backward, filling her to bursting.

"Don't you see what this is like for me?" she asks.

"I'm trying to."

"Let's turn this around. What if I had an old boyfriend that called me up all the time, and then I told him what you told Sharon. What would you feel?"

"That you're a loving person, with an open heart."

Angie steps back. Her hands are up in the air. "Boundaries, Matt. I'm talking about boundaries here." Her voice is loud and hard. The light in his eyes hardens, too. Color rises in his face and Angie is stunned by how incredibly beautiful he is. Even in her hurt and rage, she wants only to put her arms around him and hold on for dear life.

"You have to trust me," Matt says.

"Trust takes time."

"Will you give us that time?"

Her hands drop. It's freezing, and she's tired of standing there. She could remove the gift for Matt's mother that she's been carrying in her purse, hand it to him, and walk away without a word, her silence delivering her message with dignified eloquence.

"Okay."

He hugs her. She hugs him back, without the kind of warmth she longed to express only a moment before.

The day proceeds as planned. They don't talk about Sharon. They do talk more about Christmas. Matt hasn't decided yet if he's going to visit Pittsburgh. He'd rather stay in Dunston, even if Angie's tied up with her family. Angie says he can be included in the festivities, he shouldn't feel otherwise. In fact, they'll stick it out together. He appreciates her looking at it like that. He offers to help with dinner.

As a special treat, Angie adds roasted garlic to the mashed potatoes. An hour and a half later, Matt complains of heartburn. His upset stomach makes sex impossible, so they lie in bed watching a movie. Matt says garlic doesn't usually do this to him, and Angie says she put in quite a lot. She offers to go to the grocery store and get him some Tums. It's after midnight and she just wants to go to sleep. Matt says she doesn't have to, he's fine, then asks if she has a heating pad he can use. She pulls it out of her bedside table and plugs it in. She dresses, blows him a kiss, and grabs her coat. She hears him changing channels in the bedroom and wonders why he didn't say he didn't like the movie. It was an old film noir, *Out of The Past* with Robert Mitchum. Matt suggested they watch it when she surfed past. Maybe he thought *she'd* like it. Maybe it was another way of making up for what he said to Sharon.

Angie forces herself not to think about it. The store isn't far. Inside, the lights feel brighter than usual. The treads of her rubber boots squeak as she marches along, reading the overhead signs until she finds the health and beauty section. The Tums are on the top shelf, and she stands on tip-toe to see better. What flavor would Matt prefer? Wintergreen, cherry, orange, or grape? As she debates the merits of each, she hears someone whistling a familiar tune. She walks quickly to the end of the aisle to see Potter striding along with a bottle of champagne. She's tempted to go after him, but what's she going to say? That he's not allowed to celebrate whatever it is? And what is it, anyway? She hopes he and Mary Beth didn't get back together. She lingers until he's paid at the checkout counter and through the door before taking her place in line behind a teenaged boy who reeks of pot smoke. She's annoyed to see that she chose the cherry when she was certain she'd reached for the grape.

But it doesn't matter, because Matt's asleep when she gets back. On TV a shopping channel natters about non-stick cookware. She turns the TV set off and crawls into bed.

She wakes before he does. Her dreams had her searching an old house for something she left there and can't find. After that came a familiar sequence where she's trying to mail a past-due bill. First, she can't find a stamp, then she can't find a mailbox. When she tries to make her payment online, her computer won't connect to the internet.

In the living room, with the heat coming up wonderfully through the floor grates, Angie sees Matt's phone on the kitchen counter. She picks it up, turns it on, and scrolls through his text messages without the slightest sense of doing wrong. A text from Sharon, that came in the evening before when Angie was in the kitchen cooking, says *Sorry to be a pain, but I really need you, Matt*, to which Matt replied, *I really can't do this anymore. Try to understand.* Angie's chest is tight, and her hands are icy. She turns off the phone and puts it back exactly where she found it. She sits at the table, which is flooded with sunshine.

Why does she cry? Relief? Feeling foolish for yelling at him in the street? Every other thing that's made her miserable in her entire life? She calms and wipes her face on a piece of paper towel. In the bedroom, Matt sleeps on. Her legs feel heavy, so she gets back in bed, and falls asleep quickly.

chapter thirteen

Angie doesn't want to talk about Matt, so she describes the breakfast at Foster's house with Potter. Nancy commends her on being willing to help him transition out of his marriage. She wants to know how she feels about her parents living in the same house again. Angie says it's fine, it's not like they're involved romantically.

"And if they were?" Nancy asks. Her sweater is almost the same shade of blue as the one Angie put on this morning after discovering that her first choice had a stain. She's decided to bag the pantsuits for a while and try something a little more stylish. She's sure Nancy noticed the change and just didn't say so.

"Well, I guess I wouldn't like it too well."

"Why not?"

Because she doesn't want to see Potter get hurt again, should Lavinia change her mind. He's bound to be fragile after Mary Beth, though the man whistling in the store with the champagne didn't look fragile at all but brimming with confidence and happiness.

"My Dad's been through a lot," Angie says.

"And your mother? She lost her husband a couple of years ago, didn't she?"

"Yeah, but. . ."

Nancy looks at her in that quizzical way she has, by tilting her head and folding her hands in her lap in a gesture of eternal patience.

"Well, that's different," Angie says.

"Why?"

Because Lavinia is as tough as nails, though Angie has seen her be vulnerable, too. Years ago, right after she married Chip, she got

144

pregnant. She told only Angie and later brought Angie with her to the doctor's office, saying she was just in for a prenatal wellness exam. On the way home, she said she'd had an abortion. Five children were enough, she couldn't face having another. She cried. Angie was bitter about the baby—she'd wanted another sibling—and was stunned at her mother's display of weakness.

"Doesn't your mother have feelings, too?" Nancy asks.

"Of course."

"Try to think about why your father's feelings are more important to you than your mother's."

Of course, what Nancy is driving at is why the feelings of one are worth protecting, while the feelings of the other aren't. Angie supposes it's a matter of assessing damage, or preventing damage, to be exact. Potter gets hurt and he crumbles. Lavinia gets hurt, maybe a few tears are shed, and she soldiers on. Angie feels more tenderness for her father than she does for her mother, she always has. She's overlooked the pain her mother's had because she assumed she didn't *feel* it as much, but how can she know for sure?

"I just want him to be happy. For them both to be happy," Angie says.

Nancy says nothing, just goes on watching her. Angie holds her gaze. She thinks you could learn a lot about playing poker from a therapist.

When she reaches her office, Angie lifts the blinds. She has a view of the courtyard where residents gather in warm weather. One woman's family organized a birthday party for her eighty-fifth there last spring. There were balloons and bouquets of flowers, children milling about looking bored, a middle-aged son and two daughters, also looking bored. The mother, in whose honor the party was thrown, just sat, watching them all. Angie tries to recall her expression. Was it one of fondness? Derision? Or was she just as bored as everyone else, going through the motions, trying to be happy?

Angie settles in. Her first task is to try to figure out how to get Mr. Billings involved in something creative. He's in assisted living, so he's still reasonably mobile, but he doesn't like leaving his room. In the four months he's been at Lindell, he hasn't been seen anywhere except the dining hall. There have been no visitors. He has a car, and he's able to drive, but the car sits in his assigned parking space, unused. Angie pulls up his file. He was an anthropologist and spent time in the high deserts of Mexico. Maybe she could persuade him to give a talk to a small group about his experiences there. She'd have to invite residents who are still curious enough about things to ask questions, and then have a list of topics he could address in case the first few fail to pique their interest. The best outcome would be for him to simply tell a story and highlight a big moment of his career. Better yet, she can suggest that he share something funny, something unexpected.

Her phone shows the usual morning text from Matt. This one says he hopes they can have dinner tomorrow. He still hasn't decided about going to Pittsburgh. Would Angie like to go with him, if he does? On an impulse, she responds with, *Sure, why not?* It would do her good to get out of Dunston for a little while.

A woman stands in her office doorway. She's tall, elderly, and elegantly dressed in a black tailored jacket and pants. She wears a string of black and white pearls. Over her arm, she's draped a black wool coat with fur at the collar and cuffs. She asks if Angie has a moment. Angie says yes, of course.

"I'm Dorothy Firestone," the woman says. Angie stares at her, then invites her to sit. She gets up to close the door, then takes her chair. They look at each other across Angie's desk.

"You've been speaking with my sister," Dorothy says.

"Yes, about you, in fact."

"Jared told me."

"Ah."

"As you can see, I'm very much alive."

"Yes."

They pause.

"I think it's safe to say that Lillian has quite a complex about you," Angie says.

"We haven't spoken in decades."

"That's a shame."

"Perhaps I should explain."

"Please."

Dorothy says she lives in New York City. She's an architect, specializing in renovating ailing brownstones, though most of them aren't ailing any more. She officially retired about ten years before, but still likes to keep her hand in. Her voice is calm and friendly, and Angie's toes curl inside her shoes, waiting for her to say what she came to say.

"You can't imagine what it's like to grow up with someone who despises you, just for being born." Dorothy dabs her nose with a tissue. "My poor parents were oblivious. Lillian hid her feelings from them quite successfully. As far as they knew, she wasn't wild about me but had a mild degree of affection which she demonstrated by an occasional pat on the head. Of course, when they weren't looking, she hit me."

"You told on her, I imagine."

"For a while. But Lillian was a good liar. Very practiced. And they had their own problems and weren't interested. They told me to leave her alone, and everything would work itself out."

Lillian went off to college, then to medical school, married, came back to Dunston, by which time Dorothy was living in New York.

They managed to avoid each other. When their parents died within two months of one other, there was no further reason to communicate.

"That's terrible," Angie said.

"There was no good alternative."

"But why does she have your birth certificate?"

Dorothy sits up straighter in her chair. She fingers the pearls at her throat.

"I was unaware that she did. I looked for it one day and couldn't find it. I had to request a certified copy. That was years and years ago. She must have taken it when she went to medical school, or right after my parents died. Isn't it odd?"

"Yes, very."

Dorothy asks how the whole matter came to light. Angie explains about the folklore project. Dorothy closes her eyes. Angie watches her chest rise and fall. Dorothy opens her eyes and takes in Angie's office, settling on a large black and white photograph of Lake Dunston on the wall behind her.

Angie considers again Lillian's psychic state. The problem isn't her mental acuity, it's the depth of her falsehood.

As a girl, Angie went to camp one summer for two weeks in the Adirondack mountains. The other girls were typical eleven-year-olds, wild about boys, disenchanted with their parents, obsessed with their own bodies and how they might be judged. One girl, Marcy, came from a tiny town near Lake Placid and said she was at camp because her parents didn't want her anymore. Another girl said she must mean they didn't want her sitting around the house, now that school was out. Marcy said no, they were getting rid of her, putting her up for adoption. Everyone knew the story was ridiculous, but Marcy spent the whole two weeks offering details of the cruelty she endured at home, how she'd tried day by day to please her mother and father so they would keep her, bemoaning her fate, even breaking down in tears almost daily until they all believed her parents guilty of criminal behavior. The parents came to pick her up when camp was over. They were ordinary people, except for the fact that the mother was almost a foot taller than her husband. They gathered up their daughter and said how much they'd missed her. Marcy got into the car with a look of resignation, as if trying one more time to persuade her onlookers that everything she'd said was true.

In the years since, Angie has wondered about Marcy's tale. Most of it was told for fun, out of boredom, no doubt, a way to make her seem cool and arouse sympathy. Her words sometimes were delivered with such passion that it was clear she believed them herself. The ability to persuade oneself of a nonexistent truth can be powerful, sometimes dangerous in the wrong circumstances. History is full of fine examples. But Lillian doesn't want power, and she's not dangerous. She's tragic.

"I'm sure she concocted the whole thing to soothe her own guilt, not for doing you in, obviously, but for being cruel," Angie said.

"She talked to the police."

"Yes."

"Who would quickly have found no registration of my death."

"Correct."

"And assumed she was a bit off her rocker."

"Probably."

Dorothy looks worn out, not nearly as fresh as she had only a few minutes before. Angie admires her for coming all the way up from the city to talk to her in person when a phone call would have sufficed.

Jared reached out to her about ten years ago, Dorothy says. He'd grown up not knowing her, only of her. She and Jared met for the first time when most of their lives had already gone by. He wasn't particularly close to Lillian. Apparently, she'd was a difficult parent. His only brother isn't really in the picture. He moved to the West Coast right out of college. He didn't want anything to do with either

149

of his parents, and his contact with Jared has been cordial, but scant. Jared clearly wanted some extended family, though he didn't strike her as lonely. Just seeking, curious, the way artists are, she supposes.

As for her, she'd thought of looking up both boys many times. She has no children of her own. Her husband died thirteen years ago, and she's had the occasional moments of feeling adrift. Jared's presence in her life has helped with that a lot.

Her tone is sad, even regretful, and Angie feels for her.

"Why don't you go down now, and say hello? I should probably let her know you're here. To ease the shock, I guess. What do you say?"

"I've been dead to her for a long time. It's better I stay that way."

"I think it might be good for both of you if—"

"I can't. I'm sorry."

"But you've come such a long way."

"I've done what I came to do. And I've had a lovely visit with Jared."

Dorothy stand, puts on her coat, thanks Angie for her time and leaves.

Angie sits for a little, then goes down the hall to Sherry's lair and lays the whole thing out.

"The mind is a curious thing," Sherry says. She makes it clear she's not interested in discussing the matter further, so Angie shares her idea of Mr. Billings giving a talk. Sherry says it might be better to wait until they're through the holidays. Maybe in January?

Angie says that's an excellent idea.

chapter fourteen

Parking on campus is a nightmare. It's late afternoon, classes haven't let out for the day, and most of the lots are full. The temperature has fallen to twelve degrees, and Angie feels the chill inside her heated car, underneath her quilted coat, deep down in her insulated boots and thick socks. Lynn invited her to meet after her last class and to go on to dinner somewhere nearby. Angie thinks they should just have chosen a place, and met there, rather than having her navigate all the way across the quad first.

She finds an empty space in a visitor lot two buildings over. She pulls her scarf over her chin and chugs off down the salted path. The trunks of the stately elms are ringed with white lights; some windows are, too. One has lights in the shape of hot peppers, another reminder that she's far from a warm sun.

Christmas is less than two weeks away. She hates the commercial hype, the pressure to spend money, the constant failure to please. She's determined to simplify the whole thing and buy one nice gift per person. Her list is long—two parents, Alma, four siblings, Sam, and Matt. She usually gets Sherry a box of chocolates, which sits on her desk unopened well past New Year's and then gets eaten within a few days. Clearly, Sherry has no annual resolutions about improving her diet.

Matt wants a guitar and can't afford it. The one he's after is in the window of Wilson's Music, just off the Commons. The guitar is blue with white mother-of-pearl inlay. It doesn't seem like a serious instrument, but the look on Matt's face as he gazed at it says that for him it's as serious as the ground he stands on. Seven hundred dollars is a lot of money to spend on someone you're only sixty percent sure about. Well, maybe it's close to seventy percent. They've been seeing each other three or four times a week, mostly staying in because of the weather, though they took in a great film last weekend, a remake of *Jane Eyre*. Angie never got into the Brontës when she was young but knows the story by heart. Her latent sarcasm was no match for Jane's stirring self-sacrifice and honor, though her sharing her inheritance with her adopted family did seem too good to be true. She can't tell if Matt liked the movie, too. He said he did, and she decided he meant it because 1) it's not the kind of thing worth lying about and 2) she's getting tired of doubting him. That second observation has been aided greatly by the absence of Sharon unless he's silencing his phone and catching up with her later, but Angie doesn't think so.

As usual, she has no idea what to get her mother. Last year, the pale green silk scarf was accepted with mild enthusiasm. The year before that, the crystal figure of a horse seemed to remind her too much of her rocky childhood and her farrier father. Alma is easy to buy for. She likes cookbooks, especially ones with lots of cake recipes. She also likes mystery novels, though she's probably already caught up on this year's new releases. The twins go in for gift cards at high-end department stores like Saks or Neiman Marcus, though Maggie seems to have gone bohemian. Last year she wore harem pants and a peasant blouse for Christmas Eve dinner. Foster is mad about classical music, particularly Bach, so another CD is an easy buy. Timothy likes a good bottle of wine; Sam will always accept a new leather-bound journal with blank pages to scratch out her poems in; Potter enjoys plush socks or a hand-knit cardigan.

Angie trots up the steps into Kensington Hall, grateful for the warmth rising from the steam radiators. There's a lounge to the right. Lynn is on one end of a tattered couch, looking at her phone, her coat across her lap. Angie didn't think she was late, but a quick look at her own phone says she's running between ten and fifteen minutes behind.

Lynn stands up, smiles, and says, "I think he's still here, so we can go and say hello."

"Who is?"

"Professor Sanders."

At Angie's lack of recognition, Lynn says, "The folklore project? I just turned it in."

"Oh, okay, sure. Great!"

Angie takes off her coat and follows Lynn up two sets of stairs to a large lecture hall where a distinguished-looking man with silver hair sits at the desk in front, going through a stack of booklets. Her boots squeak even more loudly than they did in the grocery store the other night. The professor doesn't lift his head at the sound of their approach, no doubt accustomed to years of students coming and going around him. It's only when Lynn addresses him in a soft, deferential voice, that he looks up.

"Professor, this is my good friend, Angie Dugan. She helped with the project," Lynn says, which earns Angie a quick inspection over the top of his bifocals.

"You're at Lindell."

"Yes."

"My sister's there. Enid Slattery."

"I see."

"Do you know her?"

"I'm afraid I don't."

"She's in one of your cottages. Still quite spry." The professor smiles, revealing an expensive set of dentures.

He tells both women he looks forward to reading the oral history Lynn recorded.

"And edited," Lynn adds.

He pats the stack of bound reports at his side to indicate that Lynn's is on the top.

"Have you seen it?" he asks Angie.

"Only bits."

"I have a copy for her," Lynn says.

As a man who grew up in love with the written word in all its forms, he came late in life to a passion for the spoken tradition, he says. He got the idea for this project from his children when they were young, wanting to share something they both had experienced but only one at a time could tell. The competition to speak first and most persuasively—the power of *story*, pouring from those young lips was both touching and illuminating. This was how the human race knew itself and kept itself human. Of course, there's nothing terribly original in his understanding of story-telling—incisive texts have been penned by greater minds than his (and here he says, believe me, ladies, this is a rare admission for a scholar). The goal of the folklore project is to get students to recognize something of themselves in what they hear. Lynn, here, sought out an elderly population. Another student interviewed rape victims, looking for commonality in how the shattering event is described. And another talked to inmates, trying to amass a vocabulary unique to those behind bars.

"To learn how to *listen*, that's the key," the professor says.

Lynn glows. Angie says they should probably leave the professor to his work.

"Thank you for stopping by. I hope you both have a wonderful holiday," the professor says.

They walk to the car, and Angie asks Lynn where she wants to eat.

"I don't know. There's a place in College Town if you're into burgers and beer," she says.

"That works."

Holly's Tavern, where Matt used to work, is an academic version of The Watering Hole, with pennants on the wall and a letterman

154

jacket stapled to a corkboard. They take a table towards the back, away from the door and the freezing air that sweeps in when it opens. The server drops off two menus and walks away. Angie watches her go. It's Sharon. Angie's surprised she's working after the news of her arrest. Dunston's a small town. Everyone knows everything. Sharon didn't seem to recognize her. She never waited on her at The Watering Hole the few times Angie went there before she and Matt started going out.

Oh, thank god!

"So, how's everyone at Lindell?" Lynn asks.

"Everyone's great. Though something wild happened."

"Yeah?"

Angie shares the story of Dorothy's visit.

"Holy crap! That's amazing." Lynn turns thoughtful.

"What?" Angie asks.

"Oh, I was just wondering how that would affect my paper. I don't think it will, actually. I mean, I recorded what Lillian said, and gave my interpretation."

"Which was?"

"You know, an overwhelming sense of guilt, trying to prepare herself for the great journey ahead."

Angie suspects that Lynn is some New Age dingbat and decides it doesn't matter. There was a time when she would have cared and kept distance between them.

She drops inside herself, struck by a possibility.

"What's up?" Lynn asks.

"I was just thinking about why I went into social work."

"And?"

"Well, to help people, of course. But also because I had a bad habit of being too hard, you know, critical, judgmental. I'm the eldest of five kids, and I was very bossy."

"My eldest is bossy, too."

"You have kids?"

Lynn holds up three fingers. Sharon returns and asks if they want anything to drink besides water. Angie smiles her best smile and asks what's good on tap. Sharon names a new pale ale from Oregon. Angie and Lynn will each have one. Sharon leans across the bar and gives the order to the bartender, who brings his fingers to his lips in a clear gesture of affection. So, *that's* how she got hired. Clever girl.

"Ethan's the oldest, followed by Michelle, and then Justin. They're with my ex this week," Lynn says.

"Ah."

Sharon drops off the beers. Angie and Lynn order burgers, Angie's with bacon, Lynn's without.

"He didn't like my going back to school," Lynn says. "I'm not saying that's why we split up, but it was a definite thumb on the scale."

"Worried about the money?"

"We had plenty saved. Also, he's a lawyer, does pretty well. He said he didn't want to have to take care of the kids on his own, but I did that, even when I was working."

"So, he must have a hard time when they stay with him."

"His wife handles them."

They drink for a couple of minutes without speaking.

"I'm sorry, you were talking about going into social work," Lynn says.

"Oh, right. Well, I think I thought it would teach me how to be less harsh with people, more sensitive, if you will."

"And did it?"

"The jury's still out on that one."

Lynn laughs. The skin around her eyes crinkles charmingly. She says people don't appreciate blunt-speaking enough.

"For sure," Angie says.

"Which is why I told my ex he's a jerk for telling the kids they'd be at his place over Christmas when he had them last year. We're supposed to trade off."

"You'll be alone?"

"It's okay. My cousin and I will do something. He lives with me, which helps because he's unemployed and takes care of things at home."

"Nice."

Angie pays for dinner and drives Lynn home. She lives down in the Flats, the part of Dunston that borders the creek by downtown. Her house is one she and Matt walked past the other day, after buying his mother that owl. It's cheerful and tidy from the outside, an effect enhanced by the living room lights glowing through a layer of ice on the windows.

Back at her place, with Peggy in her lap, Angie wants to call Matt and say she saw Sharon but doing that would lift her in his mind. Angie accepts that he's moved on from her but knows he must still think of her daily. That's how it is with people you've been involved with. It takes so long for them to fade away.

In ten years, where will she and Matt be? She's deliberately not thought about their future. Staying in the present is better, more practical. That's just a way to avoid getting hurt, though. Feelings will do what they want, when they want. Any position one takes against them is often another chapter in denial.

So, what *are* her feelings?

She attempts to analyze her overpowering attraction to Matt. Is it more or less than what she felt for the others?

Stop it. That won't get you anywhere.

Peggy rolls onto her back. Angie rubs her head, causing an instant riotous purr. Peggy's little furry face is beatific.

Just enjoy it and see where it goes.

"That's what you'd do, isn't it?" Angie asks Peggy.

Angie wipes her eyes. Her tears have a life of their own these days. But she doesn't feel sad, just . . . deep, probing into herself, trying to let herself relax and just feel her growing love for Matt.

Love.

There it is.

"Shit."

She wishes she had ice cream in the house. She took herself off it a few months before. If it weren't so cold out, she'd go to the store. A night like this is meant for staying in.

She asks Peggy how she'd feel about a fire. She cleans out the grate and adds kindling and newspaper from the box she keeps next to the hearth. She brings in fresh wood from the back porch. She ordered half a cord in the fall, and if the winter keeps going the way it is, she's going to need more in another five or six weeks.

As the flames rise, she lifts Lynn's report, entitled *Our Stories, Our Lives*, from the coffee table. She flips through the pages.

Bessie Miller has this to say:

The most important thing? I'd have to say my marriage. It certainly took the most work and made getting a doctorate seem like a snap. Herbert was an easy man, but what's an easy man? Poor thing was moody, sad, troubled by things he didn't want to talk about. That's how men were in those days. You weren't supposed to spill your guts to anyone, especially not your wife.

A page later: *I couldn't tell him the truth about Jeff. He knew it in his bones, of that I'm sure. But Herbert was very traditional, 'old school,' you'd say. The word 'gay' was bad enough, but when applied to your own son, it was like poison. So I protected Jeff, I protected Herbert. That's what women do. They protect the men they love.*

Angie puts the report down. Reading it makes the winter night colder. She's lonely. A black tide of anxiety rises under her breastbone. She does her stress breathing: in-two-three-four, hold-two-three-four, out-two-three-four. She repeats until her chest hurts. Maybe she's calmer. She can't tell.

She texts Sam, *what's up?*

A few minutes later Sam writes, *studying for finals.*

Good luck!

Thx.

Matt's on shift, but she texts him anyway. *Hey.*

What's up?

Chilling.

Yeah?

Angie holds her phone without typing. Then, *I think this is going to be the coldest winter on record.*

That's what they're saying.

Really?

Yup. I gotta go. I'll call you tomorrow.

K.

She's still on edge, so she checks her voice mail at work. There's a message from Jared Firestone. He says he'll try her again in the morning, or else just swing by Lindell if that's okay.

Angie can't bear another conversation about his guilt-afflicted mother, but she'll do her duty and hear him out. That's her job.

Articulating that exhausts her, and she takes Peggy into the bedroom to sleep.

chapter fifteen

Angie doesn't want to spend her Saturday helping Potter move the rest of his stuff but agrees. Matt offers to help. Foster and Timothy are also on board to do the heavy lifting, though he's not taking any furniture, just a lot of boxes. In the years living with Mary Beth, he became a serious reader. Potter rented a pick-up truck and he thinks one load should do it.

The plan is for everyone to meet at Lavinia's for coffee. Angie tries to find a way to get out of that because she's not ready to introduce Matt to her mother, but Matt says it's no big deal, and that now is as good a time as any. Angie hopes if she follows his lead, and just takes it easy, she won't stress out too much. The minute they come up the driveway, which is now plowed, park and get out of the car, the pounding of her heart says otherwise.

Matt looks up at the house and whistles. Lavinia greets them in the kitchen. She shakes Matt's hand and says it's quite a pleasure.

"I can see why my daughter wants to keep you all to herself," she says and offers him a cigarette. He politely declines. He says he quit last year.

Lavinia takes their coats. She asks Angie if hers is new.

"No."

"Well, it's just lovely."

It's made of tightly woven alpaca, warm yet dressy, not the kind of thing one wears to load the back of a pick-up truck. She has no idea why she chose it over her down coat except that the idea of that one made her feel so blah. Another attempted sartorial boost is the ruby red wool sweater paired with the lavender scarf she recently bought.

160

Standing next to Matt, who's again in a flannel shirt and jeans, she feels middle-aged.

She realizes she doesn't know how old Matt is. It never occurred to her to ask.

Oh, crap. What's if he's younger than I am?

She chides herself for being an idiot.

Lavinia offers coffee. They accept. Alma wanders in, still in her bathrobe. Angie introduces her to Matt. Lavinia wants to know what shape Potter's room is in.

"A rectangle," Alma answers. Matt guffaws, then stops when he realizes he's the only one laughing. Alma offers to make eggs. Angie and Matt sit, and Lavinia goes into another part of the house for something. Alma takes out a can of air spray and blasts the kitchen.

"Wish to hell she'd give those damn things up," she says.

Angie scoots closer to Matt on the banquette, leans in and whispers, "This may sound silly, but I don't know how old you are."

He turns and smiles down at her. "Old enough to know better."

"Come on."

"Seriously?"

"Yeah."

"41."

"Really? You're kidding."

"No, why?"

Because someone who's 41 should have his act together a lot more than Matt does?

Internal dialogue:

Hold on there, sister, 'should have his act together?'

What do you mean? He tends bar.

So, you want him to be a doctor or something?

No, not exactly, I just thought...

Thought what? That he should be more serious?

Well . . .

Look, as long as he's serious about you, that's all that matters. Stop being such a snob. You sound like your mother.

"What planet are you on?" Alma asks her.

"What?"

"I said, do you want jam on your toast?"

"No, thank you."

"Simple enough question." Alma turns to Matt. "You must be keeping her up at night."

Angie's face burns.

"I knew it," Alma says, and sits down. "To be young again."

Matt chuckles. Angie wants to slide under the table. Lavinia returns to the kitchen. When she sees Angie she says, "You're not running a fever again, are you?"

"I never ran one."

"You were warm the other night."

"I was fine."

"Maybe it was just because you were upset."

Matt shovels his eggs in, then demolishes the toast on his plate. "What were you upset about?" he asks.

Lavinia and Angie look at each other. Angie counts to five.

"Work," she says.

"You should quit that job. A young person should be around young people," Alma says.

"The staff is young. For the most part," Angie says. Her face cools.

Matt squeezes her knee under the table. She squeezes his.

Timothy and Foster arrive. Angie introduces Foster to Matt. Foster reaches across the table to shake his hand. He and Timothy keep their coats on because they think they should get going before the snow starts up again.

Angie and Matt wriggle off the banquette, thank Alma for breakfast, and head to the hallway for their coats. Matt says he'll ride ahead with Timothy to get started. He tells Lavinia it was nice meeting her.

"Will we see you over Christmas?" Lavinia asks.

"Yes," Angie says.

"Sure," Matt says.

When he's gone, Angie thanks her mother for her discretion earlier.

"I wasn't about to tell him you're having second thoughts," she says.

"I'm not having second thoughts!"

"Good, because he's gorgeous."

"Mom!"

"What? I'm not dead yet."

Angie slips into her coat. She stands before the mirror across from the closet while she zips it closed.

"Do I look old?" she asks.

Lavinia stands beside her, considering their reflection.

"*I* look old," she says.

"No, you don't."

"Thank you, dear."

Angie pulls on her gloves, then her hat.

"He's 41," she says.

"Who? Matt?"

"Yeah."

"So?"

"So, nothing."

Lavinia says 41 is a great age for a man, an age when you can start to take him seriously. Angie promises to keep that in mind.

The mood is somber at Potter and Mary Beth's. The guys work in silence, or with only a few words, "Here," and "I got that." Potter is still packing his books. His clothes and personal items went over earlier that morning, which means he got an early start. Angie stands in the doorway to the guest room he's been using, watching him scan the spines of the books he puts tenderly in the box.

He sees her and nods. Angie hears crying coming from the master bedroom at the end of the hall. She takes off her coat, leaves it in the room where Potter is working and walks along the thick carpeting to the double doors at the end. She knocks lightly. The crying continues. She knocks again. When there is still no answer, she opens the right-hand door and sticks her head into the room.

Mary Beth sits on the bed in her bathrobe and slippers. She looks small and tired.

"Mary Beth?"

Mary Beth turns her blotchy face Angie's way. She shows no surprise at Angie being in her bedroom.

"You're part of the clean-out crew," she says.

"Yes."

Angie takes a few steps closer to the bed. The lamps on the bedside tables are modern and heavy, with metal circles and squares inlaid in black enamel. The headboard is covered in black fabric, raw silk maybe. The sheets are black, too. Potter and Mary Beth went to Las Vegas on their honeymoon, and she clearly drew inspiration from their hotel room.

"He doesn't have to go, you know. I'm not seeing Jason anymore. I broke that off," Mary Beth says.

"I see."

"It was never as big a deal as Potter thinks it was."

"Since when is cheating on your husband not a big deal?"

Mary Beth blows her nose into a piece of Kleenex she's been holding in her hand.

"He's not easy to live with," she says. "He gets moody. Withdraws. Won't tell me what he's thinking about. It makes me . . . lonely, left out."

Mary Beth pushes her hair back from her face.

"You meet a man, you spend time with him, a lot of time, you think you really know him, what makes him tick. You get married, you try really hard. You lift him up, give him a job, encourage him every single day, and then you find out you don't know him at all."

"I should probably go."

Mary Beth stares at the floor and says nothing. Angie leaves as quietly as she can.

The mood lightens as the day goes on. The boxes are unloaded at Lavinia's, Potter treats everyone to pizza and beer. Timothy has to leave to meet Sam downtown. She's got her eye on a lamp she wants him to look at. Foster needs to get back to Mad Max. Matt arranged to take the whole day off, and he and Angie head back to her place. Angie opens a bottle of wine, lights a fire, puts a Bach cello concerto on the CD player, and settles on the couch next to him.

"You think he'll be happy there?" Matt asks, meaning Potter at Lavinia's.

"For a while. Until he disappears."

"You mean, leaves?"

"No, just turns inward. He does that."

Matt nods, then sips his wine and sighs. "Alma's a character."

"Yeah."

"I like your mom."

"She likes you."

They stare at the fire. Angie loses herself in the elegant logic of the music. What must it be like to possess the kind of talent that lets you compose this?

Angie asks Matt if he's ever written songs. He says he used to, when he was younger, and might again, one day.

She looks at him. "I want to know everything about you."

"I've told you the important stuff."

"Tell me the unimportant stuff."

He looks at her with a curious gleam in his eye and puts his glass of wine on the coffee table.

He was born in Pittsburgh, which she probably figured. His mom was only 20 when she had him; his parents got married a couple of years after he was born. His father didn't see the need since they were living together happily enough, baby in tow, but his mother insisted. It wasn't that she felt ashamed of not being married, she just wanted that extra commitment. He thinks it was more about the token of commitment. His sister was born when he was 11. Because of the difference in their ages, it's really as if they both grew up as only children. Jen didn't know their father well because their parents split up when she was only a year old. Matt has thought about the timing of their separation a lot. He finds it hard to understand what would make a man leave a baby. He probably never wanted a second child and found it to be too much responsibility. His mother says it was she who wanted another one, to bring them closer together, meaning there was already trouble between them before Jen was in the picture. That never works, does it? Thinking a baby will make your relationship healthy again.

166

"I don't know," Angie says.

Things were hard after the divorce. His mother taught, but her salary was meager, and his father didn't help much. He quickly formed another family with a woman he'd been seeing on and off while he was with Matt's mother. He was a long-haul truck driver and wasn't in the area all that often, which made pressuring him to make his alimony payments difficult. Matt took care of Jen a lot if his mother had to stay late for a meeting or a parent-teacher conference, at least until he went to college.

"You went to college?" Angie asks.

"Yeah, right here. Dunston University." Matt reads her expression. "Surprised that an Ivy League graduate tends bar?"

"No, I just didn't know, that's all. What did you major in?

"English literature."

"Wow."

"Yeah, wrote my Honors Thesis on James Joyce."

"I'm impressed."

Matt shrugs.

He says she's probably wondering how he afforded school and says he got a scholarship. It didn't cover everything, so he had to work, which is when he discovered how much fun bars can be. After college, he got back into music, played with a few bands, but they always broke up for one reason or another, usually an artistic difference or someone's drug problem. In one case, the drug problem was his. He was into cocaine in a big way. He thought it helped his creativity. That was when he was also trying to become a writer, but nothing he wrote was any good. In his mind, the songs he composed were better. He couldn't convince anyone to perform them. He reached a point when he had to stop the cocaine, had to get out of Dunston for a while, so he relocated to Tennessee.

"Nashville?"

"Good guess."

He got clean, worked in several bars, most of which were also performance venues, and still couldn't get on stage. He was disappointed, angry, depressed, and started drinking too much. Then he had to wrestle with that demon, and the whole thing left him in bad shape.

The woman he was involved with at the time helped him a lot. Sue was nine years older, steady as a rock until she found the love of her life and moved on.

"That must have been awful," Angie says.

"It was, but I got over it."

He came back to Dunston because it was the only place he ever felt a real connection to. He found a room in a house with a bunch of other people. They were a mixed group, some in professional jobs— one guy was a paralegal, another was a bookkeeper—but most were like him, working ordinary jobs that weren't super challenging. Eventually, he wanted his own space. That's when he moved into the apartment he has now. He got a job where Timothy works. After a while, they became friends. Retail wasn't for him, so he went back to serving drinks.

"When was this?"

"About a year and a half ago."

"And don't you ever wish... I don't know."

"That I'd done things differently? Sure, sometimes, but you can't change the past."

"True."

She has to know, though, is it really enough, tending bar? He says ambition can be a bad thing if you can't handle disappointment. He's not bored with his job, he digs the music aspect—did he say he'd followed up on Sam's idea and asked Gus if he could take on booking the gigs? A bluegrass band is coming in next month. He doesn't want the bar to get known as leaning too much towards one kind of music. Maybe after a while, if there were a strong preference from the audience, he'll move it in a clear direction.

Angie wishes she'd encouraged him to talk to Gus. She's had plenty of chances. Does she want him to remain just as he is, and not evolve? She'll have to work that out with Nancy, or better yet, by herself, but now isn't the time.

"And your own stuff—writing, songs, are you working on anything?" she asks.

He shakes his head.

"That part of you is still alive, though, right?"

"Always."

"Maybe you just need someone to believe in you."

He looks at her. "Maybe I do."

She puts down her glass, and lifts her hands as if to say, *Ta-Da!*

"Blind faith can be another bad thing," he says.

"Nothing wrong with these eyes."

She leans in and kisses him. A little later, she takes him to bed.

chapter sixteen

The Christmas tree in the lobby leans noticeably to the right. Sherry's mentioned it several times; Angie's left a message for Raoul, head of the maintenance department, twice; the receptionist thought she'd do everyone a favor, tried her hand at pulling it straight, and tipped it over. She and Angie managed to get it back up. Now Angie rehangs the ornaments, which are white and gold spheres in varying sizes. There are no garlands or tinsel. The lights are also white and the only thing that stayed put when the tree went down. She gets a stool from the utility closet down a side hall and perches on it to put the star at the top. She steps down from the stool and stands back. If anything, the tree leans more than it did before.

Each resident's doorway is lined with a paper chain garland, donated by the local elementary school. Most are red, some are green. One rebellious child made his in yellow, and Angie chose that one for her office. On her desk sits a tiny plastic tree with blinking lights. She's had it for years and installed it just that morning.

Jared Firestone finally followed up on his earlier message and said he has something to give her. She returns his call, leaves a message, and says she'll be in all day.

The morning's snow stops around ten-thirty, and sudden sunshine cascades through her office window. She stands a moment by the glass, hoping for some warmth on her skin, and finds none. She walks the resident halls, leaning into rooms, asking how everyone is. Mr. Jenkins is in one of the common areas, parked in his wheelchair in front of a large birdcage with chattering finches. He wears a Santa hat. The nurse on duty says his grandson is supposed to visit later that day. His expression is morose. A small wrapped gift is perched in his lap. Angie greets him and asks if he would like her to take charge of the package so he can eat lunch without worrying about it. He looks down and doesn't seem to recognize the box. Then he says he rather hang onto it if that's okay.

Jared appears at twelve-thirty sharp. Under his arm, he has a canvas wrapped in brown paper. Angie holds it while he removes his coat. He smells of the outdoors, and something spicy, like aftershave. He's wearing a dark green cardigan and gray slacks. His knuckles have splotches of color on them, white and gray paint is visible under several fingernails on both hands.

He tells her to remove the paper and see what she thinks. It's the painting he was working on when she visited his studio. The small blue dot has taken on its own life and became a wild swirl dominating the muted tones around it.

"It's beautiful," Angie says, and gestures for him to sit.

"Thank you. I think our conversation brought out the best in it."

Angie thinks the swirl might represent Lillian. Or the effect of Lillian's tall tale on Jared.

"Are you really sure you want to give it away?" Angie asks.

"Yes."

She offers him coffee and then says the cafeteria tends to let it sit a long time in the pot, so it might not be the best. He says he's fine. He really can't stay long, anyway, because he's on his way down to visit Lillian.

"I encouraged Dorothy to, but she declined," Angie said.

"Too much water under that bridge."

Jared says it was just so odd growing up, knowing there was this aunt somewhere in the world. When he and his brother asked about her, Lillian wouldn't say a thing. Their father went along with it—he was probably more circumspect about that situation than he should have been. Jared doesn't have children of his own, but if he did, he'd want them to have the full picture of their extended family.

"She would have had to explain her animosity," Angie says.

"She's not the kind of person who can state her own faults well."

His brother has two children, and they've seen Jared off and on over the years, although the brothers aren't particularly close.

"He could never accept my lifestyle," Jared says. But he admires his brother for putting his own objections aside enough to have let his children know him.

Angie looks again at the picture, which she's propped up against the wall. She thinks she'll hang it over the fireplace. Jared sees where she's looking and asks her what the picture makes her think of.

"Winter."

"Full of howling wind."

"Exactly."

Jared says he wants to move somewhere warm, and will after Lillian is gone. Florida perhaps.

"That sounds nice," Angie says.

They went once, the whole family. Years ago, of course. They drove, and his father didn't like the hours behind the wheel, so he tried to persuade his mother to get rid of the car and fly the rest of the way. Or take a train. Or a bus. By then he didn't care.

"And?" Angie asks.

"We just kept going. We got there, eventually."

"Was the ocean lovely?"

"Yes. It reminded me of breathing."

They conclude the interview. Jared wishes her a merry Christmas. Angie wishes him the same.

After work, Angie heads down to the music store to see about that guitar for Matt. She's tried to draw him out about brands and styles as subtly as she can and hasn't gotten very far. She asks the guy at the

172

counter if she can return it. He says sure, just make sure it's in the same condition it was when it left the shop.

"Acoustic or electric?" the clerk asks.

"Uh, I don't know."

"Well, what are you into?"

"It's for my boyfriend. I don't know what he likes to play. He hasn't played for a while."

"Probably acoustic then."

"Is that blue one acoustic?" Angie asks, meaning the instrument in the front window.

"Yup." The clerk is on the late side of middle-age, heavy, and moves slowly, as if in pain. When he lifts the guitar, he holds it lovingly, gently. He hands it to her. Angie takes it.

"I don't play," she says and hands it back.

The clerk strums the strings, tunes it, then plays a short classical piece Angie recognizes but can't name.

"You're really good!" Angie says.

"I used to be."

"Don't play anymore?"

"Not really."

"That's too bad."

He taught himself when he was a kid, he says. That was the sixties, everyone played guitar, or so it seemed. Then he went to Vietnam, and when he came home, he didn't want to play again until he had grandchildren. They couldn't tell how rusty he was, but listening to himself, he thought it was a shame he'd let so much time go by. He tried to get back into it the way he had before, but something had gone out of him. He likes to think he can pick it up again if he really wants to, that's what his wife always says, but that day hasn't come around yet. Maybe he's just too old now.

"No, you're not. Trust me, I work at Lindell, and you're not even close," Angie says.

"Just for that, I'll knock twenty bucks off the price."

"Much appreciated!"

She buys the case to go with it, and a replacement set of strings. He offers to carry the guitar to her car, but she can manage. It's not heavy, and she likes the feel of it in her hand. At home, she stashes the guitar in the closet and realizes that wrapping it will be impossible. She brings the painting in from the car. She removes her collection of small crystal figurines from the mantle, her favorite of which is an elephant, and props the painting against the chimney. It looks wonderful.

Matt calls and asks if she wants to come down to the bar and help him decorate the tree. Finals are in full swing, and he thinks they'll have the place pretty much to themselves. She says she'll be right down. She gets into a sweatshirt and jeans. No effort to look good today, she thinks. It's just too cold outside.

The tree at The Watering Hole is huge, probably nine or ten feet tall. Matt's got a box out and is removing ornaments, many of which are broken. Angie gets to work, too. She strings the lights. When she plugs them in, about half the bulbs stay dark. There's no one in the place except the cook, who pokes his head out and asks if anyone's hungry. Matt asks him to slap a couple of burgers on the grill.

"On the house," he tells Angie.

"Where's Gus?"

"Visiting family out-of-state."

"And you're in charge."

"That how I got stuck with the tree."

They break off and sit at the bar with the two beers Matt just poured out. He says he's been trying to dig up some financing.

"For what?"

He gestures with his arm in a wide sweep.

"You want to buy the bar?"

"Yeah. Gus said he's going to be putting it up for sale in the spring. He's been wanting to retire, and the bust must have moved up his timeline."

"Wow."

He's talking to the bank soon. He's got financial statements put together. He's good with dollars and cents. The problem is his own credit rating isn't so great, because he got in trouble a while ago with his credit cards.

"That happens to a lot of people," Angie says.

"A lot of people aren't asking for the kind of money it would take to make this place mine."

The burgers come out, and they eat. The door opens, someone walks across the bar. Before they can turn, Sharon is at Matt's side. She's pale, and Angie thinks she's been crying.

Matt pushes away his half-eaten dinner.

"What's up?" he asks.

"I've been looking for you," Sharon says.

"I've been right here."

Sharon looks at Angie. Angie looks back. Does Sharon recognize her from the other night? She gives no sign. The skin of the back of Angie's neck tingles. She feels just the way she used to, with some pushy kid on the playground, right before she threw the first punch.

Sharon climbs up onto a stool. "Can I get a drink?" she asks Matt.

"We're open."

"I wasn't sure. It's dead in here."

Angie closes her eyes and folds her hands across her chest. Matt laughs. Sharon doesn't.

Matt asks what she's having. Sharon says vodka, straight up. Matt walks around the bar and holds up the Stolichnaya. She nods. He pours it, she knocks it back. She puts the glass on the counter. Her hand is still around it.

She says she came to say good-bye, that she's leaving Dunston.

"What about the trial?" Matt asks.

Sharon shrugs.

"You can't just skip out."

"Yeah?"

"You'll lose your bail."

"Wasn't my money."

"Whose?"

"Gus."

"They'll come after you."

"Only if they find me."

"Sharon, come on."

Angie gets off her stool and returns to the tree. She removes the defective light string. There's another one in the box. She plugs it in, first. When all the lights light, she wraps it around and around. It only covers the top third. She decorates that same portion with a weird mix of ornaments—some are spheres, as one would expect, then there's a Santa Claus, a princess, a palm tree, and a plastic shoe. She admires her handiwork. Sharon and Matt are still sitting. Their body language says the conversation is difficult. Matt leans closer to her, his mouth just above her ear.

Angie approaches. She leans on the bar next to Sharon.

"You should go," she says.

"What?"

"Get out."

Matt says nothing.

"Who do you think you are?" Sharon asks.

"Someone who's telling you to leave, and not come back. Wasn't that your plan, anyway?"

Matt still says nothing.

Sharon slides off her stool. She doesn't offer to pay for her drink. She looks at Matt. Matt shrugs. His expression is a blend of fury and grief. Then she's gone.

"Why did you do that?" Matt asks.

"Someone had to."

Matt's off his stool now, too, looking down at her. Angie doesn't like his eyes. He steps back, putting distance between them.

"I told you, there is nothing going on between us," Matt said.

"I'm not saying there is."

"So, why did you tell her to leave?"

"Because she's a god-damned pain in the ass."

"So are you."

"Whoa, what's this?"

Then they're yelling. He says she can't tell other people what to do. She says he's been played for a fool. At that, his hand comes down hard on the bar. He says if he's been a fool about anyone, it's her. There are more words, but Angie loses track. Something pent up inside of both of them runs wild. Neither of them can catch it. She grabs her coat and is out the door. He doesn't come after her. She walks to her car without putting her coat on, not feeling the cold, not caring if she freezes to death, there on the sidewalk. In her car, with the engine on, staring through the thin layer of ice that formed in her absence, she sits, feeling the rage slip away. In its place is a hole that bewilderment and regret quickly fill.

She takes out her phone. There's a message from Lynn; another from Potter. She can't listen to them now. She can go back to the bar, but what would she say?

She cries, hoping Matt will appear, but he has no idea where she parked.

She stops crying and wipes her face.

She waits until she can't wait any longer. She drives home, collapses on the couch, and weeps herself dry.

After a period of time that could have been minutes or an hour, perhaps even longer, she opens a can of soup and thinks back to the burger she barely touched. The soup is lukewarm and salty. She realizes it's split pea with ham, never her favorite. Why did she buy it, then? Had she been trying to persuade herself that it was a wise choice? How can something you can't stand ever be a wise choice? She forces herself to eat what's in the bowl, puts it in the sink, rinses out the pan, and stretches out on the couch. Her face is hot, and her hands are cold. So are her feet. She grabs the soft throw she keeps neatly folded on the back of the couch and tosses it over her legs. She lies on her side, facing into the room, and focuses on her breathing. When she wakes up it's well after midnight. Peggy is curled up behind her knees. Angie feels a surge of affection for her constant presence, loyalty, unconditional love, all things she hoped to receive from Matt and now never will.

She sits up. Maybe she shouldn't have ordered Sharon from the bar. She probably wouldn't have stayed too much longer, in any case. Matt's right, it wasn't up to her to bully her like that. But after all this time, with her hanging around in the periphery, Angie snapped. And then the old mean girl came out in full-force.

She looks at her phone. No new calls, no texts. She taps in his number and stops.

She undresses and slides into bed. Tomorrow everything will sort itself out.

Only it doesn't. Angie pours herself into work, which means making sure the Christmas spirit pervades everything until even the most withdrawn residents enjoy the piped-in carols. The staff all wear Christmas tree pins. The nurse in Lorna Green's memory care hall even pins one on her. Lorna doesn't know the difference, and Angie doesn't have the heart to remind the nurse that Lorna is Jewish. She doesn't have the heart for anything. Her limbs are heavy and slow. In the Ladies' room after lunch, she decides she hates her hair, though it's as thick and shiny as ever. She schedules an appointment for after work. Her stylist hasn't seen her for a while and asks what she's got in mind.

Angie says she wants bangs and a bob. The stylist says ever since Michele Obama got hers, bangs have been really in. She takes her to the washbowl, leans her back, and drenches her head with water that's almost too hot. Angie says nothing and figures this discomfort will buy her some small forgiveness, either for her recent transgression, or one in the future, of which there will be no doubt many. The stylist natters about her annual Christmas trauma. Her husband's parents live in Vermont, which sounds like a lovely place to spend the holidays, right? Only their house is ancient. The windows leak air, the appliances in the kitchen are about fifty years old, and making dinner is a super challenge. Her husband loves the place, thinks it's rustic and quaint, but then he's never in the kitchen. He's not the one boiling potatoes on a gas stove that has trouble staying lit or roasting a bird in an oven whose thermometer has no bearing on reality. She's not kidding. One year she brought up one of those thermometers you hang on one of the racks, and she noted a difference of over thirty degrees. She left it there, safe in a drawer, but the next year she couldn't find it. Anyway, her mother-in-law has mobility problems, and her sister-in-law—the husband's brother's wife—doesn't do anything but sit on her butt and scream at her kids, who hide in the grandparents' bedroom with the TV on all the time. So, who ends up in the kitchen? That's right, yours truly.

Her scissors snip, Angie's hair collects on the floor. She regards herself in the mirror. Her smock has a pattern of pink flowers that reminds her of the gowns you put on at the doctor's office. As her hair shortens and lies more closely around her face, she despairs of her choice. She recalls being six years old, and her father, in an attempt to do something useful, lined all the kids up and cut their hair. It was a nice idea, except he was three sheets to the wind. Only Angie's came out reasonably well. Everyone else had dramatically uneven hairlines. Their mother berated him for days. As the stylist puts on the finishing touches, Angie's new bangs give her an innocent, even hopeful air, as if she could wish upon a star and have everything work out just right. She watches her eyes moisten. The stylist doesn't notice. She's busy running product through Angie's hair, pinching and plumping. The mousse smells too sweet, like a flower about to rot. The stylist removes the smock, hands her a mirror, and turns her chair around so she can appreciate the back. Matt would say how different she looks. He might say he didn't recognize her at first. Then he'd say he doesn't like the new cut, that she was fine before. That's not the kind of thing Matt would say. Or is it? Since the blowup, she feels she doesn't know him, never really knew him.

He's probably thinking the same thing about me.

So, that's it, then? They met as strangers, and parted the same way?

The thought of going home suffocates. Peggy can wait another hour for dinner, so Angie drives. A light snow falls. She goes out to the lake, pulls into the parking lot, turns off her headlights, and looks out into the dark. The breaking waves are rhythmic lines of white. She imagines the water, the unbearable temperature of it, the restlessness, the weeds below the surface, the bottom littered with sunken boats, the items thrown overboard too heavy to float, a few bodies, too, though the fish have probably feasted on them long ago.

Jeff Williams drowned the summer she was in sixth grade. He was a classmate, an ordinary boy with a crew cut, which set him apart because no one else wore them. His parents owned a sailboat, and the boom swung around and hit him from behind. He knew how to swim, so it was thought the impact knocked him out. Divers went down, but the lake is very deep; no trace of him was ever found. Angie couldn't look at the lake the same way after that. Even on the calmest, sunniest day, the flat blue held menace.

She turns on her lights and leaves the parking lot. On the road back to town, she takes a curve a little too fast and skids. She turns her wheel in the direction of the slide and straightens out. She comes close to ending up in the ditch. She slows down. It's hard to hold the wheel because her hands are shaking. She refuses to cry.

At home, she draws a bath in the neglected tub. The rumbles in her stomach remind her that dinner is overdue. Once again, she hasn't gone to the store. There's probably some frozen meal she can microwave.

The water is tepid by the time she stands up, but she is much more relaxed than she had been. Baths will be on her daily docket starting tomorrow. A comforting routine is crucial if she's going to get through this.

The freezer yields nothing of interest, so she orders a pizza. The chipper voice on the other end of the phone says it will be about forty-five minutes.

Dressed in her beloved sweatpants, sweatshirt, and slippers, she cleans out the grate and lays a fire. Seated before it, with a large glass of wine at her side, she lights a match. The kindling is dry, almost eager, and the flame spreads. Has she ever looked at fire and found it joyous? Or just defined by its own nature, rising in hunger, or even rage? Energy released, that's what makes fire.

And love.

The wine goes quickly, but she won't have another glass. It would be so easy just to get tipsy, then drunk, and fall asleep. But the morning light would be thin, the day cold, her heart sore, and her head pounding. Some faraway place, that's what she needs. Sherry reminded her just the other day about all the vacation time she's got accrued. Hawaii? She could swing that, though it would put a dent in her savings. Then again, the money's not doing her any good, just sitting there.

With her laptop on her stretched-out legs, she searches for flights. January seems to be a popular time to go, seats are already booking fast. Then there's the matter of a place to stay. She finds a resort on Maui whose cheapest room is over four hundred dollars a night. A more modest hotel? No way. If she's going to escape, she's going to do it in style.

The pizza comes, she devours two pieces, then resumes her online search. Photo after photo shows a happy bride and groom standing on a white-sand beach, the turquoise ocean at their backs.

Grief washes over her so strongly her body feels like lead. The night's chill penetrates, and not even the fire's roar can warm her. It's been approximately twenty-seven hours since she strode out of The Watering Hole, but her heart says it's been more like six months. If she hadn't lost her cool, what would she be doing right now? Hanging out with Matt, or surfing the net just as she's been, only the getaways would include him, and she'd assess everything on her screen in terms of whether or not he would like it. Yesterday was her point of no return, the thing she can never take back, like the man who slugs his kid and finds his life forever changed.

She finally listens to her voice messages from the day before. Lynn thanks her for the other evening and wishes her a very happy holiday season. Potter says he's settling in fine at Lavinia's, and that she should thank Matt for his help the other day.

Matt's absence from her life is going to raise questions she doesn't want to answer. She needs a point man, someone to share the news and instruct everyone to leave her alone. She dreads the forced, artificial atmosphere this will create during the pending family gatherings and hopes that there will be enough people to lightly turn the conversation in other directions.

It's late, but Angie calls her mother anyway. Lavinia doesn't answer until after the fourth ring but sounds awake and alert.

"What's wrong?" her mother asks. Lavinia recently opted for a caller ID feature because Alma complained of too many scam callers.

"I broke up with Matt."

"When?"

"Yesterday."

"Why?"

Angie describes the scene at the bar. When she gets to the part about Sharon, Lavinia laughs and says, "Good girl!"

"He got really mad at me," Angie says.

"You caught him off guard."

"We said awful things."

"That's typical."

Lavinia says she hears regret in her voice. "So, which of you called it quits?"

"Neither of us. I don't think. I can't really remember."

"No, 'I don't ever want to see you again,' or 'Leave me alone?'"

"No."

"You didn't break up. You had a fight."

Really? Is that all?

"I haven't heard from him," Angie says.

"He's probably embarrassed. Have you called him?"

183

"No."

"So you're both being stubborn."

Her mother may be right.

"I don't know what to do," Angie says.

"Sleep on it. I need to get to bed, myself."

Angie thanks her. Her mother says not to be too bull-headed, or she'll put the kibosh on the whole thing.

The fire is low now, the embers a lovely orange. Staring at them, drawn to their glow, Angie knows *this* is what she feels, and that there's no point in denying it. It scares the hell out of her and probably always will.

The call to Matt goes to voice mail. He could be closing the bar; he might be at home, already in bed. The idea that he's with Sharon darts in like a hungry bird after a spider. She sends the bird away. His voice on the recording fills her with joy, pain, overlain with lust. A poet couldn't have described it better. The recording ends, she doesn't speak. No words come.

Then, "I love you."

She hangs up.

chapter seventeen

The staff luncheon drags on. Sherry ran the risk of offending Lindell's chef by hiring a local caterer. Her explanation, delivered in her easy, lilting tone is that he had his hands full with next week's holiday menus. He comes in late and sits, not enjoying himself until he samples the smoked salmon, which he declares to be superb.

Angie positions herself by the door in case it all gets to be too much, and she needs to bolt. Her nerves have been soaked in scalding water. Matt hasn't called, texted, dropped by, sent up a flare, a smokescreen, enlisted the aid of a carrier pigeon or been in touch in any way since her confession two nights before.

It's inexcusable. Her heart is broken; her soul brims with rage. She opened herself to him, and he slammed her shut. Just like that. With clenched fists and gritted teeth, she survives until the weekend.

On Saturday morning, she fills Peggy's food bowl and changes her litter box. It's early, the sun barely above the horizon. It will take just under five hours to reach Manhattan and the high-end stores on Fifth Avenue. She'll park at the Port Authority and take a cab from there. She's following the logistical advice of her sister, Marta, who's lived in New York for five years. In a rare mood of generosity, Marta offered to help Angie shop. What's she looking for, anyway?

Angie doesn't know. Something. Everything. A luxurious sweater. A stylish new coat. With her longed-for tropical vacation now tabled, she's ready to dip into her savings account. Her anxious brain reminds her that she was thinking of leaving Lindell, taking a year off, finding a new venture that all those thousands of dollars are going to guarantee. Her angry brain says to hell with it, she's not getting any younger.

By the time she eases up the narrow, winding ramp to the parking garage's top-level, she's exhausted. Traffic crawled through the

185

Holland Tunnel. On the street, it's impossible to hail a cab, so she walks, six long blocks across the center of the island until she hits Fifth. The sidewalks are mobbed with holiday shoppers. Everyone looks so fancy. She's never seen so many fur coats in one place. Her feet are sweat-soaked inside her insulated boots. How is she supposed to try on shoes?

She ducks into a Starbucks and asks for the drip of the day and a muffin. The coffee's too hot, the muffin stale, and there's nowhere to sit. A young guy wearing red earbuds gets up suddenly as if he's just remembered he has somewhere to be. She drops into the vacated seat. Outside the window, the river of pedestrians is relentless, flowing in both directions. Car horns sound several times a minute. The noise level inside is high, too. The couple at the next table are arguing about the best place to buy Joey's gift. Angie imagines Joey is their French Bulldog. He wears a bow tie and beret. No one looks at her, even though she's laughing to herself. New Yorkers have seen it all.

What's Matt doing right now? Thinking how pathetic she is? Glad that he's finally rid of her? Or does he feel bad, too, and wishes things had gone differently?

"Screw that," Angie says.

She chokes down the muffin and leaves.

The display windows at Saks are a glory of winter scenes. Pink, glittering cotton frames plastic women clad in silks, furs, shiny brocades. Angie is mesmerized until she looks into their empty eyes. She also doesn't like the visible seam at the neck and wrist. A detachable hand is unsettling, a detachable head even more so, but then all of their body parts are removable, right? And hasn't she wished from time to time that she could change out what she's got for something better? Maybe what scrapes is being reminded how trapped in her own self she really is, but *that's* a thought that will ruin the day, if she dwells on it.

For once, Marta is on time, standing by the perfume counter, just where she said she'd be. She's dressed in a red leather coat with fur cuffs and collar. Her cross-body bag is also leather, but navy blue, making her look both sleek and incredibly stylish. Marta had some success with her acting in the last year, and for once her confidence matches her outfit.

They embrace. Marta says the new hair cut suits her, but that she seems tired. Angie blames it on her early start. Marta asks if there's a special occasion she's come down to shop for, a special party or dinner, perhaps with the new boyfriend?

"How do you know I have a boyfriend?"

"Mom told me. Then Dad did, too."

"Big news, because it's such a rare occurrence."

"That's not it at all. They're just happy for you."

"Yeah, well, we broke up."

"Already? Pisser."

Angie lifts a small cut-glass bottle from the counter. She sprays the air and leans forward. She's instantly assaulted by a sickening scent of spiced orange.

They take an escalator up a couple of floors. Marta seems to have the store's layout memorized. If it's cashmere Angie's after, she knows right where to go. They get off the escalator and pass a headless mannequin in a sequined bodysuit, display tables, round racks of clothing, bitter-looking women burdened with coats over their arms and bags in each hand, and come to a quiet corner near the back where they're suddenly the only customers. On a table are sweaters piled neatly in several bright colors. Angie touches one. It's incredibly soft. The tag, showing a handwritten price of eleven hundred dollars explains why they're alone. Angie says she can't afford it, and Marta says yes she can. Last Christmas, Angie made the mistake of mentioning her account balance when Marta asked point-blank what it was. Marta has always pried. Nothing is private. Maybe that's the result of being an identical twin.

Angie tries on the purple one. She expects the sweater to make her look fat, but it slims her. The way the fabric touches her skin is almost erotic. She sits on the stool in the dressing room and curls her toes inside her stuffy boots to keep from crying. It doesn't work, but the tears pass quickly. She emerges and says she'll take the sweater. Marta looks at her closely but makes no remark.

Angie doesn't buy anything else, but Marta picks up a pair of leather boots, a scarf, and some lime-green eye shadow she says she needs for a part.

"Don't they supply all that?" Angie asks.

"I have a unique interpretation of my character."

Angie doesn't ask her to clarify. Marta invites her to lunch. She knows a quiet French place.

"Since where are you into French food?" Angie asks.

"Since my director bought me dinner."

Marta's fey tone suggests a growing relationship, but again, Angie doesn't pursue it.

The restaurant is over on Madison, looks unassuming from the outside, and sits down a short flight of stairs from the sidewalk. Inside is a sea of red and gold, small crystal vases holding white flowers on each table, soft lighting, mellow jazz on the sound system. The other patrons are mostly older women, elegantly dressed in tailored jackets and slacks, wearing a lot of jewelry. Pearls seem to be everyone's favorite. This is not a place for the budget-minded.

Angie gobbles down her quiche, and Marta picks at her salad. She's wearing a silk blouse with a deep V-neck which shows off her emerald pendant to advantage. Angie doesn't have to ask if the stone is real. Marta doesn't wear imitation anything. They're drinking white wine, getting loose, almost happy. Marta asks if Angie thinks it's weird that their father has moved in with their mother. Angie says nothing those two do ever strikes her as weird. She tells Marta about finding

Mary Beth in tears the day Potter moved out. Marta shrugs, suggesting that Mary Beth's grief is well-earned.

Angie's phone rings. Their table is in a corner, so she thinks it's okay to answer it, though the waiter is looking at her with disapproval.

"Listen, I just got a new phone because I pitched my other one at the wall after you left that day. Yeah, I know, stupid right? Broke the damn thing. I've been trying to get it fixed and they finally said it had to be replaced, so here I am."

"Matt?"

"Yeah?"

"What the hell?"

"What the hell what?"

"You called."

"Yeah, and I would have tried you at work, but I figured you didn't want to hear from me there. I mean, boundaries, you know? So they moved over all my contacts and messages over from the old phone and I saw you left one. I haven't listened to it yet. I hope you didn't tell me to get lost."

"I didn't."

"Sorry I didn't get back to you before. And I'm sorry for what I said, but I've been under all this pressure with the loan thing—the bank doesn't think they can do it, so I talked to my mom, and she can't do it, either. I've been scrambling."

She says nothing. Marta's looking at her own phone. The waiter, in black slacks, black jacket, and white bow ties, pours them each more wine.

"You there?" Matt asks.

"Jesus."

"What?"

"What did you say?"

"When?"

"At the bar."

"That I was a fool for you."

"What did I say?"

"That I was an asshole."

That's it?

Here she is, thinking she told him to drive a nail into his head, jump into the gorge, or swallow bleach.

"I thought we broke up," she says. Marta lifts her eyes.

"Really? Because we fought?"

"Yeah."

There follows another long pause. Angie hears him breathe.

"Do you *want* to break up?" he asks.

"No."

"Me neither."

She says she's in the city, shopping and having lunch. She won't be back until late. He can come over if he wants. He says he does.

When she hangs up, she drinks her wine. Marta looks at her.

"So, you're back together," she says.

"I don't think we were ever apart."

"Except in your own head."

One blow-up, one broken phone, and a reluctance to call her at work added up to the worst personal catastrophe in the last five years. And it wasn't even real.

I love you.

What will he think when he hears that?

"Are you all right over there? You look like you're about to have a stroke," Marta says.

"I'm fine. It's just warm in here."

They finish lunch, and Marta pays. Marta's going to keep shopping and says she'll be up next weekend for Christmas. Outside the store, a man in a Santa suit rings a bell by a hanging Salvation Army donation kettle. Angie digs in her wallet for a couple of bucks when Marta stops her.

"Don't. They're anti-gay," she says.

Angie puts her wallet away and thanks Marta again for lunch. She watches her sister walk off, swinging her shopping bags, weaving in and out of the crowd, until she's gone.

Angie has no trouble hailing a cab. She doesn't want to think her luck has changed because of Matt. She doesn't want to think about luck at all, only her own agency, which at the moment involves getting out of the parking garage, back through that infernal tunnel, and on the road to Dunston.

Alone in the car, she feels stupid for not reaching out to him sooner. She went through a boatload of misery for no reason. Stubbornness can get you through a lot of bad things, but it can also get you into just as many. She'll have to work on that.

Later, when the winter afternoon is a blend of purple and gray, snow falls. Within the hour, she can barely see. Her tires are good, she knows she can make it home, but she's exhausted from the long day and the relief over Matt.

As she descends the Pocono Mountains, where her speed averages around forty miles an hour, she comes into a small snow-covered town with a diner. She wants to sit still for a few minutes where it's warm and bright. Hers is the only car in the parking lot and she wonders if the diner is closed, but the lights are on, and a figure sits at the counter, hunched over what looks like a newspaper.

She's met by a delicious smell of frying meat which instantly returns her to The Watering Hole. A stupid spat, that's all it was! He missed her, probably wondered if she'd moved on in her heart. Did she? She not in exactly the same place. Maybe he's not, either.

The woman behind the counter wears a holiday sweater decorated with embroidered candy canes. Her earrings are in the shape of tiny bells. Her face isn't cheerful, just business-like. She hands Angie a menu.

"Can I get breakfast?" she asks.

"Sure."

Angie wants two eggs over easy with hash browns, bacon, and toast. What happened to her diet? She'll hit the gym an extra day this week. Or she'll shovel out her driveway—that's even better than using the elliptical. Or she'll ask Matt to go skiing again, then reviews what a disaster that was before. She bets he'd stay with her this time, though.

The man who's been at the other end of the counter leaves. A blast of cold air rushes through the door. The waitress pours Angie a cup of coffee she didn't ask for and says they're saying it's going to be the coldest winter on record.

"Maybe it's another ice age again," Angie says.

"What happened to global warming?"

"That just means there's more energy in the atmosphere. Weather gets more extreme."

"Gotcha."

Angie watches the snow fall, brightened by the outside lights. Snowflakes have six sides, and each has a unique pattern. How can that be? It's been a long time since she was inspired by the world of nature. People forget how to look at things, she thinks. How to *experience* them.

Her plate comes. She dips the toast into a shiny yellow yolk and eats. If she were stranded on a desert island, and could only have one dish, fried eggs and toast would be it. She decides against the hash browns, thinking again of calories. Matt's never said anything about her weight, but then any mention of it would be disastrously awkward. In bed, he treats her body with respect, and also as if he can't get enough of it.

Her phone rings. It's Sam, saying she's sorry she's been sucked down by finals, but they're over now and her head's clear.

"That's great!"

"Where are you? You sound funny."

"Milton, PA. In a diner. Eating eggs."

"Why?"

Angie explains. Sam says it takes a lot of guts to brave Manhattan during the Christmas rush. Angie says it was fun. She needed a break. They pause. Angie hopes Sam doesn't ask why the break was necessary. She doesn't. Instead, she says Mary Beth has been calling Potter a couple of times a day, according to Timothy.

"What's she want?" Angie asks.

"Him back."

"Oh, god. Seriously?"

"That's what Potter says."

Maybe she's afraid to be alone, or her pride's hurt, or she thinks Lavinia might just win, after all. Or maybe she really loves him. So why did she stray? What was she looking for? What wasn't Potter giving her that drove her to someone else?

"Why are relationships so complicated?" Angie asks.

"Because people are complicated."

"Spoken like a poet."

"Ha!"

Sam asks if Angie ever got ahold of Lillian's son. Angie tells her the story. Sam says it's pretty wild, a whole invented tale, but maybe then again, not so wild, given what her own mother told her all those years ago about her father.

Angie says she better get on the road. They hang up.

The plows have been out, and she makes better time, but it's close to nine when she pulls into her driveway. Peggy greets her coolly. She doesn't like being abandoned for a whole day. Angie removes her boots gratefully, then her socks, and lets her feet breathe.

For the balance of the drive, she forced herself not to think about Matt, which was easy, given how challenging the road was. But now, safe at home, he fills her in a way that exhausts her. After days of longing and remorse, she needs to sleep alone.

He answers her call on the first ring. She says she's beat. Is he off tomorrow? He is. She tells him to come around noon and to plan to stay over. She'll get to the store and stock up. The news says they're in for another foot, at least.

"You sure you're okay?" he asks.

"Yes. Why?"

"No reason."

She waits. He must have heard her message by now.

"Matt—"

"What?"

"Nothing."

They wait again.

"Me, too," he says.

She turns away from the window where she's been standing, as if someone out there could see her wild grin.

"You, too, what?" she asks.

"You know."

"Okay."

Her bed doesn't feel lonely. His presence is almost palpable. And of course, there's Peggy, under the covers, purring madly, to keep her company.

chapter eighteen

Sunday mornings are always quiet in Angie's corner of the Heights, this one is silent. The light that creeps past the edges of her bedroom's blackout blinds is a blend of silver and white. She knows the sky is a solid mass of gray, without an inch of blue, and that it will remain that way until the day is swallowed by night.

Her sleep was fitful; the roundtrip drive to the city was long. What was she thinking? She wasn't thinking, only feeling, a bad mix of anger and despair.

Despite the trials of the day before, she is suffused with peace. She still has Matt. She won't ever do anything to jeopardize that again. That means learning to hold her tongue.

"Well, better late than never," she informs Peggy, who during the dark hours relocated herself from under the covers to the pillow next to Angie's.

She showers, dresses, and postpones coffee until after she has gone to the store. Lavinia left a message asking if she needed her to go for her—she made this offer to Timothy and Foster, too—given her all-wheel-drive (she really does think Angie should look into getting one). The message came in at 6:46 a.m. Her mother is still the early riser she always was. Angie texts back that she's fine, but thanks, in fact, she's on her way out now.

A good eight inches fell overnight. Angie is glad her driveway is flat. The road beyond is flat, too, recently plowed, but new snow is accumulating fast. Cruising up and down the store aisles, she is filled with delightful anticipation of the day ahead. She's going to dump a hunk of beef in her crockpot and roast up a bunch of carrots and potatoes. She's also going to bake bread, assuming Alma can be enlisted to tell her the steps over the phone. Candles are a nice touch, but she'll

196

have to dig out the crystal candlesticks her mother gave her one year and wash them carefully, by hand. And there must be wine, really *good* wine, two bottles even, because who knows? In vino veritas and all that, though Angie already feels the truth and suspects Matt does, too. They're meant for each other.

She buys enough food for a week, although the snow is supposed to taper by evening. At home, with everything put away and the crockpot on the counter at the ready, she makes sure all is tidy, neat, and welcoming. Peggy watches her flit about from room to room and refuses to rouse herself, though she's been known to trot madly, in response to Angie's sudden bursts of energy.

She wears the new sweater and a pair of stylish jeans she bought the year before and couldn't quite squeeze into. She's shocked that they fit well. When did she lose weight? Nancy had suggested that she stop weighing herself, and focus instead on what she's eating and when, and to determine if she's truly hungry before she even takes a bite. It must have worked! She's not used to good things happening without her constant attention. Maggie, now all new-agey and bohemian, would say it's a gift from the universe.

The beef goes in the pot; the vegetables are clean, sliced, and ready for the oven in a couple of hours. Alma's instructions on bread-making were clear, delivered without a single question about why Angie has decided this day to bake, and after mixing and kneading—which she again enjoyed a great deal—the ball of dough sits in a bowl under a damp towel, rising joyously. The classical music station plays nothing but Mozart. The DJ comments dryly on the weather and warns everyone out there to take care.

Just past one, Angie's mood slips from calm to annoyed. She calls Matt, he doesn't answer. Her message is cheerful. She hopes the snow isn't giving him trouble, and if it is, she can come get him.

"I can get through anything," she says, realizing she meant road conditions, but that he might take that another way.

An hour later, he still isn't there and hasn't called.

Jerk!

Her heart steels. She opens one of the bottles of wine she bought. She pours herself a generous glass, and silently toasts her solitary future.

A car comes up the driveway. She doesn't have to look to know it's Matt. He's over two hours late. He knocks. She waits until he knocks a second time before going to the door. She carries her wine with her, with a fleeting idea of throwing it his face. She opens the door and he walks in past her, not stamping his boots on the mat, tracking snow right into the living room she vacuumed just that morning. He flops down on the couch, with his coat and gloves still on. She smells liquor. She puts her glass on the coffee table and stands before him until he lifts his sick-looking eyes.

"Something happened," he says, his voice thick.

"Clearly."

He takes off his gloves, then wriggles out of his coat.

"Well?" she asks.

He pats the couch next to him. She drops down, leans back, and crosses her arms.

"Jen OD'd. She's okay, in the hospital, but it's been touch and go for the last day. I just found out this morning when my mother called. She's taking it with her usual grit. I don't how she can be so calm."

"Where is she?"

"At home."

"No, I mean Jen. In the hospital *where*?"

"Pittsburgh."

Angie's relieved. If she were there in Dunston, Matt would no doubt want to see her, and Angie doesn't want to venture forth in all this snow just to stand at the bedside of some stranger.

"Has this happened before?" she asks.

"Yeah. Twice."

"So, why…?"

"Did I have a couple of shots? I needed to take the edge off."

Angie gets up to check her dough. It's not rising the way it should, it's just sitting there in the bowl, a stupid white blob.

"You should have called me," she says, still in the kitchen.

"I know."

"I might have been able to help."

"You're helping now."

She leaves the kitchen and returns to the couch. He looks solid, yet vulnerable. Tough, yet full of pain.

She runs her hand down the back of his head.

"Hey, it'll be okay," she says.

He nods and looks completely miserable.

"She's an addict, Matt. This is what addicts do."

He looks at her. The only thing the same about his eyes is the color. The whites are glassy, the lids heavy. The thick lashes below are clotted, as if with tears that dried some time before.

She asks him to please explain just why he's taking this so hard. It's not like she died, right? He just said she's done it before. Why is this time different?

He shrugs.

"Do you feel responsible somehow?" she asks.

His silence says he does. Angie has talked to scores of people who feel guilty about bringing their parents to Lindell. She knows how hard it can be to turn over care to someone else. She always says they have to be fair to themselves and be honest about their own limitations in terms of how much time they have to devote to someone who needs more help than they can reasonably give.

"I turned her away," he says.

"What choice did you have?"

"None."

"So stop feeling so bad."

"Just like that."

"Well, no, but at least *try*."

"You don't think I have?"

Angie tries a different tack. What if the last time she came to him he gave her money, even set her up with a job, maybe at The Watering Hole, and she accepted everything with the promise that this time for sure she'd get it together, seek help, be a different person, and still failed in the end? Would her overdose have been his fault then? And obviously, his denying her money didn't slow her down one bit, because where did she get the drugs that landed her in the hospital? She knows how to get what she needs, that's for sure. What she wants him to understand is that none of this has anything to do with him.

"Except I love her," he says.

"Yeah, but you can't *fix* her."

Matt says she doesn't understand. He's known for years he can't change a single thing about her. That doesn't stop him from, what's the word he's looking for here, *grieving*.

"Do you always drink when you grieve?" she asks.

"No."

She asks if he's eaten. He shakes his head. She makes him a piece of toast and says dinner won't be for a couple more hours. Does he want to lie down? He'd rather just hang out with her if that's okay.

"I asked you over, didn't I?" She tries to sound jovial but thinks her words have an edge.

She checks the bread. It's ready to be rolled out, shaped, put in the rectangular pan she bought especially for that purpose. She invites

Matt to join her in the kitchen while she works. He gets off the couch slowly, as if his legs don't work right. He sits in the kitchen, with the window at his back. With his dark hair and black turtleneck, the white background makes a compelling tableau.

"Can you make me some coffee?" he asks.

"Sure."

She pours out what was left from the morning, rinses the pot, adds ground coffee from the bag she keeps in the freezer, then returns to her bread. She loves the feel of it, and she presses it gently into the pan. She tells Matt she can see why people get into baking. She's even tempted to make cookies and bring them over to Lindell.

"You do enough for those people," he says.

"It's my job."

"Making cookies?"

"Considering what makes people happy."

He looks at her skeptically and says nothing. Irritation rises. She pats the dough lovingly.

"I'm sorry. I shouldn't have said that," he says.

"You're upset about your sister."

Angie puts the pan in the oven. When the coffee is ready, she pours Matt a cup. She asks how he takes it. He takes it black.

She sits with him. His lifts the cup with a steady hand. He sips the coffee.

"You look different," he says.

"I cut my hair."

"So you did."

"Like it?"

"Sure."

Peggy wanders in and waits at the back door. Angie tells her she won't like it out there, stands up, and lets her out. Matt asks where she got the painting over the fireplace. She explains about Jared.

"Oh, yeah. That lady you were telling me about." The coffee has put order in his face. He's no longer slack as if he's about to crumble altogether.

He asks what she's got in the slow-cooker.

"Pot roast."

"I like pot roast."

"I thought you might."

"I like you, too."

"I'm glad."

He puts the cup in the saucer and takes her hand. He says he's sorry they got into it the other day. It left him feeling pretty bad. Then he says he wishes he were coping with his sister's situation better and that he's grateful to Angie for being so rational all the time.

"I'm not. Look what I did with Sharon."

"You were completely rational. You wanted her gone, you said so, and she went."

Angie hasn't thought of it that way.

"Well, what about when I freaked out skiing?" she asks.

"A new situation can unnerve even the best of us."

Angie wishes she could take his compliments with grace, but she's suspicious. She wonders why he's talking about her strength of character, all of a sudden.

Because he needs to lean on me now.

She squeezes his hand. She says when the bread comes out, they should build a snowman.

"It's been a few decades since I did that," he says.

202

"Me, too."

When the bread is golden and gives off a rich, earthy scent, Angie puts the pan on the stove. Peggy scratches on the door. Angie opens it, and Peggy charges in and disappears into the bedroom.

It takes a few minutes for Angie to pull on a sweater, another pair of socks, and her heavy boots. After she's in her coat, she wraps a scarf around her face, tugs on her hat and mittens. She confirms that she has her keys. There's no reason to take her purse.

The snow is almost knee-deep as they trudge deep into the back yard. The surface glitters though there is no sun to speak of, only light. They go all the way back to the fence separating her yard from the neighbors, where a stand of tall spruce casts lavender shadows. They stop. As Angie bends forward to grab snow with both hands, Matt embraces her. She clutches him. He leans in for a kiss. He tastes of coffee. He hasn't shaved, and his stubble burns her lower lip.

"Thank you," he whispers.

"Anytime," she says, not whispering.

"I don't know what I'd do without you."

Drink yourself silly?

Why do sharp thoughts rush in so easily?

Because he disappointed me.

They let each other go. Angie gathers snow, slams her hands together. She puts the compacted mass on the ground and piles more snow into it from both sides. Matt stands, watching the trees. He says there's a bird in there, hopping from branch to branch. Angie says it's probably trying to stay warm. When she's built the base, and Matt's still not helping, she suggests they make snow angels instead. Before he answers, she's on her back, the snow cradling her. It falls on her face. Moving her arms and legs is hard because the snow is wet and heavy, but she persists. She lies, spread-eagled for a moment, eyes shut, letting her mind drift. She hears nothing but the blood thudding in her ears.

She wants to depart the moment and return gently, so she may proceed with care.

She supposes all couples go through this sooner or later. Some crisis occurs and how they navigate it guides how they deal with the next one. She doesn't really care about Matt's sister; in fact, she thinks the woman sounds like a complete loser, but Matt's devotion to her keeps her tongue still. Her job is to support him, help him. She worries because as she summons the future, the sister appears as a recurring blight that Matt rushes to eradicate. Then again, if he *didn't* care about her, if his heart were hardened against her, that wouldn't be any good, either. She can't love a man with a hard heart. Been there, done that.

"I just need the t-shirt," she says.

"What?"

"Nothing. Help me up."

Standing, she brushes the snow from her legs. She asks if he wants to make a snow angel, and he says no, it's too cold, and he needs to use the bathroom, so they lumber back towards the house.

The afternoon glides effortlessly. Angie roasts her vegetables. They switch from classical music to jazz. His phone rings. It's his mother. He takes the call in the spare room, the one Potter used all those years before. When he emerges, he looks tired but in possession of himself. He says Jen's out of danger and has agreed to rehab. He also says his mother is taking out a loan to pay for it, which is why she can't help him buy the bar. Angie says she thought his mother had already passed on that. Matt says yes, true, but this was the reason why.

"She knew Jen would agree to rehab?" Angie asks.

"I guess they talked about it."

"And maybe Jen wanted one last party before she got clean."

"Could be."

Angie asks how he feels about that.

"About what?"

"Your sister getting help while your dreams go on hold."

He shrugs. He'll just have to figure something else out. Angie asks how much he needs.

"The down payment is around a hundred and fifty grand. Mom would have given me around thirty. She has a line of credit on her house."

"What about the rest? Where would you have gotten that?"

"Good question."

"Doesn't sound like you've really thought this through."

He says he's thought about it a great deal, he just doesn't have any good answers. He'd hate to see someone else get the place, but it's probably going to end up that way.

"How much to buy it outright?" Angie asks.

"Seven fifty."

"That's a chunk of change."

"No kidding."

They eat. The food is delicious. Angie's proud of herself. Matt says she's amazing. He didn't realize how hungry he was. They finish the bottle of wine, and she wonders if they should open the other one. As if to help make up her mind, Matt says he really didn't have that much to drink before he came over, just two quick shots down at the bar. He even remembered to put money in the till for them. After the wine is open, Angie says they need to let it breathe. She asks Matt to light a fire. He remembers that he brought a carton of ice cream and left it in the car.

"What flavor?" she asks.

"Chocolate."

"Excellent."

He tells her to grab his car keys from the pocket of his coat while he works on the fire unless she wants him to go. She tells him to stay put.

She opens the closet door, puts her hand in the nearest pocket of his coat, and finds nothing but a small plastic bag. It has a zip lock across the top. It also contains about a tablespoon of white powder. She checks the other pocket and finds his keys. She leaves them there. A weight settles in her stomach. She leans against the door jamb. She hears Matt in the living room, shoveling the ash into the metal bucket she keeps by the hearth, then putting fresh logs in, moving them this way and that. It's so hard to turn around and make herself walk back to him. He's crouched before the fire, watching the flames take hold. He's far away, lost in thought, and doesn't notice her standing beside him. She has the baggie in her hand and extends her arm until it's just inches from his face.

When he sees it, he says, "Oh, Angie."

He stands up, looks down at her, his eyes pleading. She drops the baggie on the coffee table and sits on the couch. He goes on standing, neither of them speaks. She won't look at him, but she knows he's still looking at her.

"It's not what you think. I didn't even remember it was there," he says.

"Sure."

"You have to believe me."

"Why?"

"Because it's the truth."

"Cocaine, I assume?"

"Yes."

"So, you're still using."

"No! I just said I forgot it was there."

206

"Matt. It's winter. It's cold outside. You wear that coat all the time. How the hell did you not know what's in the pocket?"

"Because I never use that one. The keys are in the *right-hand* pocket."

He joins her on the couch. She asks if he got the cocaine from Sharon. He says he did.

"You told me you didn't even know she was dealing. That it came as a big surprise."

"I didn't know she was dealing at the *bar*."

Angie's almost certain he said something different at the time. She puts her face in her hands. He touches her shoulder. It takes a great deal of strength to tolerate his touch.

"So, why did you buy it from her if you're not using anymore?" she asks.

"I didn't buy it. She gave it to me."

"Why?"

"I think she was trying to say thank you."

"For what?"

"I gave her money."

"*What?*"

It wasn't much, just a hundred bucks to tide her over. She was out of work. She still had to make rent. Angie says she works at Holly's Tavern in College Town. Matt's look of surprise is genuine, followed quickly by an equally genuine glare of irritation. He says he was always straight with her. There was no reason for her not to be straight with him. Then he says it occurs to him that she may have come by The Watering Hole to ask for the coke back. She might have needed to sell it if she were leaving town. Only Angie gave her the boot before she had a chance to.

"Why did she thank you with coke? Did you tell her you used to be into it?" Angie asks.

"Yes."

Angie remembers Sharon's miserable, pinched face, and hopes she's having a really bad time, wherever she is.

"This money you gave her, was it a loan or a gift?" she asks.

"A loan."

"That you'll never get back."

"Probably not."

"You know, if you're going to become a business owner, you have to get way more careful with money."

"I know."

He takes her hand. Then he puts his arm around her and draws her in. The fire rises, driven by its own rules, its own needs.

She pulls away and picks up the baggie.

"Why did you keep it, if you're not using anymore?" she asks.

"I don't know."

"Then you won't mind if I get rid of it."

He says nothing, but his whole body tenses. He stares at the fire. There is no peace in his gaze. Only anguish. She looks at him until he meets her eye. She shakes her head. She takes the baggie into the bathroom, empties the contents into the toilet, and flushes. She throws the baggie into the trash can under the sink.

"I would have done that if you hadn't," he says when she returns.

"I know."

She finds herself looking up at Jared's painting and the cold blue swirl of winter. Everything feels harder this time of year. So many obstacles. So many things to watch out for. And every year, about now, summer feels like a dream, something that can't possibly return.

"Thank you for understanding," Matt says.

"About what?"

"Everything."

"I'm not sure I do."

He nods. He says he supposes that's to be expected.

The wind rises, and rushes down the chimney, causing a mad dance among the flames. Matt says he bets the whole town will be closed tomorrow. Angie says she doesn't have to get over to Lindell unless it's an emergency.

The thought of the snow-bound residents depresses her, though she's not sure why. She returns to the idea of changing her life, leaving her job, finding something else to do. She needs a new chapter, a new focus.

"How about that ice cream?" Matt asks.

"Maybe later."

In bed, after he's asleep, with the dark all around her, she recalls his face when she said she'd get rid of the coke. An old longing? The memory of that glittering, transient joy as it flew up his nose? It may always be there, years from now. He may always be tempted.

And what of his opening up the bar to have a couple of belts to ease the pain of his sister's disaster? Will he do that every time something awful happens?

She knows people don't come with guarantees. You have to have faith in their better nature. You can only hope they'll be stronger next time. She doesn't know if Matt will be, or if she'll be patient enough—understanding enough—to help him through.

chapter nineteen

When Nancy asks how things are, Angie tells her that Matt's sister overdosed on meth, which made him show up late at her place. But things went okay. They had a pretty decent day. He stayed until Monday afternoon. Angie's learned from so many hours in his company that she's not ready to think about living together, though he's pretty helpful when it comes to chores. He did the dishes on Sunday and Monday after breakfast. He even offered to shovel her driveway, but she said he didn't have to.

"How is the sister now?" Nancy asks.

"Better."

"Good."

"He'd been drinking when he came over."

"Because he was upset about the sister."

"Yes."

"Well, we know that substance abuse runs in families."

Angie realizes she been rationalizing Matt's behavior. She has to admit now that taking a couple of shots of liquor in response to distressing news isn't something everyone does.

"I also found a packet of cocaine in his coat pocket," she says.

"You'd better fill me in on that."

Angie does. She says she flushed it down the toilet, and that Matt thanked her for doing so.

"Do you accept his explanation?" Nancy says.

"About what?"

"Why he had it in his coat."

Angie says yes, she does. She lay awake a long time Sunday night, thinking about it all.

Nancy says she seems to have gone from having an issue with trust to trusting perhaps too much. Angie says she doesn't trust too much. She just finds his words reasonable.

"And is being reasonable enough?" Nancy asks.

"For a good relationship? Yes, I think so."

"What about being reliable?"

"Reliable means different things to different people."

"As long as you're okay with what it means to you."

Angie knows she's not okay with that. She also knows she cares for Matt a great deal, more than she's expressed to him. Her instinct again is to hold back. Otherwise, she'll be lost. She keeps this to herself.

Nancy allows the silence to continue. It's her way of letting Angie regroup and find a balance.

After a few minutes, she asks how things are going with her parents.

"Well, Dad's wife got pretty weepy when he moved out. And she's been calling him a lot, apparently."

"Sounds like she has second thoughts."

"Yeah."

Angie says she was probably too hasty when she started the relationship with that other guy, that she was acting out of frustration. People have to be more self-aware, she says. Otherwise, they cause harm.

"Very true," Nancy says.

Nancy wants her to think about the upcoming family gatherings, and what she should be on the alert for.

"Oh, I imagine it will be the usual. Foster will withdraw, Timothy will be bombastic about something, the twins will be squirrelly, Sam will be a rock, Alma, too. Mom, I don't know. That all depends on Dad."

"And Matt?"

"I guess he'll be figuring out how to fit in."

"Holidays bring out the best and worst in people."

"I know all that."

Nancy shares a personal story about her brother, who tends to get morose over Christmas, sullen even, snapping at people. Their father died around then, years and years before, and this sadness became a part of him, something that both defined and accentuated him if that makes sense. She and her other brother always try to cheer him up, the way their father would have, she supposes, and it never works. After a while they just leave him alone, let him have his bad mood, his private reflections, whatever they are because he never divulges exactly what he's thinking about. It's possible he might not even know. She and the other brother spoke once or twice about excluding him, on the basis of these moods, but they never have. The sad brother's wife pitches in, too, in the efforts to cheer him, and so do his children, but sometimes it ends up being a marathon after which everyone is exhausted.

Then Nancy asks if Matt will go home to see his own family. Angie says she thinks not for a few months, until things get sorted out with his sister. As she mentions this, it occurs to her that Matt talked a lot about feeling responsible for Jen, and now, when he has a chance to see her, he said he wanted to wait. It's probably his way of protecting himself, keeping a safe distance. You can care a lot about someone and still choose to avoid their drama. Again, she keeps all of this to herself. Angie and Nancy wish one another happy holidays.

It's a short week at work because of the snow day, and also because Friday is Christmas Eve, which Angie traditionally takes off. After Matt

212

left yesterday, she went to the store and got ingredients to bake three dozen chocolate chip cookies from scratch. She didn't find it as much fun as baking bread, but she stuck with it, and only helped herself to one of the finished products. Now she has two large plates to take around to the residents and staff. She likes the idea of sharing her labor with others. The staff help themselves. Some of the residents allow Angie to put one on their meal tray or bedside table. Others wave her away.

She's not sure she wants to go into Lillian's room but knows it's wrong to exclude her. As always, Lillian is planted before her TV. The volume is off and Angie says hello. Lillian turns her head, her eyes look tired. Angie offers her a cookie, and Lillian leans to look at the plate.

"Don't mind if I do," she says and helps herself to four. She puts them in her lap.

Angie wishes her a very merry Christmas.

"You saw my son," Lillian says.

"Yes. And your sister."

"You must think I'm insane."

"No, I don't think that at all."

"I'm sure by now you realize that a living person can be dead to someone else."

"Yes."

"I tried with her, you know, year after year."

"Of course."

"She wouldn't have it. Wouldn't forgive me. Never let me off the hook. So, I suppose, I had to persuade myself that I'd done something much more awful than I really had to make sense of it all."

"I think that's very perceptive."

"Well, I think it's stupid."

Lillian bites into a cookie. She clearly enjoys it a lot, from the calm, almost greedy expression that settles on her face. She finishes it and bites into a second.

"He gave you a painting," Lillian says, with her mouth full.

"Yes. It's very lovely."

"I'm not surprised. He's enormously gifted, my Jared."

"I couldn't agree more."

Lillian finishes the second cookie, considers a third, and pauses. She looks at Angie.

"There's something different about you," she says.

"I cut my hair."

"Well, if you'll permit me to say so, I'm not sure it entirely suits you, but then again, it's not bad, either."

Angie thanks her for her candor, puts a fifth cookie in her lap, and goes on her way.

The weather has stayed clear for almost a whole day, and her office is awash in sunshine. Matt calls. Angie lets it go to voice mail. A few minutes later she listens to his message. He thanks her for the nice time over at her place, and again for being so understanding. He also says Gus has decided to let him manage the bar for the next few months, and that he's postponing selling it until then. Matt thinks this is Gus's way of giving him more time to get his finances in order, but as Angie must recall from what he told her, that's a really long shot at this point. Not unless of course, her mother happens to be looking for a business opportunity. She was in business before, right? Selling something, he can't remember just what she said.

Angie is pretty sure he remembers just fine, and that he's downplaying all this, making it sound like it just occurred to him to approach her mother, or better yet have her broach the topic, and sure enough, he concludes by saying, "If you think it's even doable, feel free to bring it up with her. If not, then obviously don't bother. Talk to you soon. Love you."

I love you too, you stinker.

She's supposed to have dinner down at The Watering Hole. Matt invited Sam and Timothy, too. He didn't ask her if she thought it were a good idea, he just went ahead. She thinks his initiative is a good thing, the result of her confronting him with his drug-using past, standing by him, and not calling it quits.

Or, maybe his energized, optimistic state has nothing to do with her. Maybe he's just relieved that his sister is going to be okay and will finally get some solid help.

The Watering Hole is empty except for a table in the back where a couple sits over a pitcher of beer. The tree Angie and Matt partially decorated a week before sports a full set of ornaments and lights. There's a green garland hung behind the bar, and a string of white lights on the bar itself. In the front windows are stick-on images of Frosty, Santa and his reindeer, and a demure angel gazing lovingly down at the manger. Angie wonders when Matt did all this. During the time when he was out of touch because of his broken phone? Or since he stayed over at her place? She realizes it makes no difference. All that matters is the spirit he brought to it all.

Sam and Timothy aren't there yet. Matt helps her off with her coat and tells her he really likes her hair.

"You saw it the other day," she says.

"I know."

Jackson's behind the bar, and Angie asks Matt why he didn't go home for Christmas. Matt says Jackson's a local. Jackson nods at Angie, and she nods back. Matt asks if she wants a booth or a table. She prefers a booth. They slide in, on opposite sides.

"Listen, I asked Timothy and Sam to come a half-hour later," Matt says.

"Why?"

"So I could give you this."

He slides a small box across the table. The wrapping paper is poorly folded, and the bow is so loose it's sliding off. Angie says she thought they agreed to exchange gifts on Christmas Eve, at her mother's place. He says he knows, but he wants to give this to her in private and hopes that's okay. She says it is but doesn't reach for the box until he nudges it a little closer to her.

She removes the paper. The box is covered in black velvet and inside is a gold chain with a diamond pendant in the shape of a heart. The stones are good-sized, and Angie calculates that he probably spent at least fifteen hundred dollars, probably more. She takes out the necklace and holds it up, watching the diamonds catch and throw the light.

"Matt," she says. She sets the pendant loosely back in the box.

"Aren't you going to put it on?"

"Sure."

The clasp is small and hard to manage, so she asks him for help. He gets up and comes around behind her. She feels a slight tremble in his hands, and her mind goes instantly to something that shouldn't be in his system. But his demeanor is sober. He's just nervous. When he's done, she removes the small mirror she keeps in her purse and looks at her reflection. The chain is long enough to accommodate her turtleneck sweater. She has to admit, the pendant is very pretty, though it's not something she would normally wear. She's not much of a girlie girl. Is Matt trying to make her over? Does he find her unfeminine in any way? She closes her eyes for a moment in an effort to silence her inane inquiry.

He sits back down. Jackson comes over and asks what they want to drink.

"Champagne," Matt says. Angie laughs and says he must be kidding.

"Don't you like champagne?" he asks.

"Sure, but beer is fine. Or wine."

"The beer is better here," Jackson says. He has a bruise under his eye Angie hadn't noticed before. She remembers Matt mentioned that he belongs to a fraternity. Those two facts probably aren't connected, but then, given what she's heard about frats from her own brother Timothy, who was in one for a while, maybe they are.

Both Angie and Matt ask for an IPA on draft. After Jackson leaves, Angie says, "I'm afraid you spent way too much money on this."

"You're worth it."

"No doubt, but if you want to own this bar one day, you need to save your pennies and not buy your girlfriend expensive gifts."

"Don't you like it?"

"Of course I like it. I'm just thinking of you."

"Well, when I saw it at the jewelry store, I was thinking of *you*."

Angie raises her hands in surrender. When she lowers them, Matt takes one and kisses it. She asks what's gotten into him.

"I might be in love," he says.

"Have you seen a doctor?"

She immediately regrets her words when the warmth in Matt's eye cools. She says she's just kidding, and that she's been in a weird mood all day. She says he shouldn't pay any attention to her and that she *loves* her gift.

"I'm glad. You deserve it," he says.

The conversation lags. She tells him about baking cookies and sharing them around Lindell. She figures that even the most withdrawn, crabby resident could appreciate a tasty cookie. He says nothing. She says Lillian Firestone took four, gobbled down a couple, and was candid about her wild tale.

"If you worked here, you'd be dealing with a younger crowd," Matt says.

"I'd be on my feet a lot more. I'm not sure I'd like that."

The beers come, and they clink mugs. As they sip, Angie realizes Matt is being serious.

"You're saying if I quit Lindell, I should work here?" she asks.

"Only after I buy it."

She says that would be a big step. He says not as big a step as him becoming the new owner. She then says she doesn't know if talking to her mother is a good idea. Sometimes she can be weird about money.

"You said she had tons," Matt says.

"I'm sure I didn't say that."

"Well, maybe Timothy did. Only in passing."

Angie wonders how long Matt has been hatching this scheme of Lavinia becoming his benefactor. Did seeing the house the other day make the idea more solid in his mind? Over the years she's lived there, Lavinia has put a lot of beautiful things in every room. When you're not used to money, it's easy to be impressed with that kind of thing.

Timothy and Sam show up. Angie and Matt slide over so they can sit. Sam sits next to Angie. Sam notices her hair right away and says it looks good. Then she sees the pendant. She says she assumes it's from Matt, and when Angie nods, Sam tells Matt he has good taste.

"In jewelry and in women," Matt says.

"Here, here," Angie says.

Jackson takes Timothy and Sam's drink order. Timothy wants a martini. So does Sam. Angie says they're so retro.

She asks how Sam's visit with her father went. Sam says it was better than she expected. She tried not to be uptight about anything, which a couple of glasses of wine helped.

"A couple? You came back smashed," Timothy says.

"I wouldn't say smashed, just loose," Sam says.

The talk turns to Christmas Eve at Lavinia's. Timothy called her the other day, and she said Potter was on the straight and narrow. Angie she says her mother can really crack the whip when she wants to, and Timothy says it's actually Alma who's keeping an eye on him. Angie can see that. Alma would treat Potter as just another child underfoot, without appealing to reason or some sense of self-respect. If she found him sneaking a snort from the cart in the den, she'd walk over and take the glass out of his hand, the way she used to when she found Foster helping himself to the chocolate milk he wasn't supposed to have until bedtime.

They all try the red beans and rice, a new dish on the menu. It's pretty good but too salty. Kevin, the cook, tends to go heavy on the spices in general, and Matt says he'll bring it up with him. Angie has to admit Matt already sounds like someone in charge. But telling people what to do and how to do it better isn't the same as keeping an eye on the bottom line.

They have a second round, and Sam gets giggly. Timothy says she'll have to learn how to hold her liquor.

"Nonsense. Bacchus and poets are best friends," she says. She announces that one of her poems will be published in a small literary journal run by a college in New England. A round of applause follows. Timothy blows her a kiss. Matt gets quiet. Maybe he's thinking about his days as a bright English major, though he never mentioned being interested in poetry. Maybe he wishes he'd followed through on the novel he tried to write. He's had his share of missteps, and forgone opportunities. Angie begins to see why owning the bar is so important to him.

219

A large party comes in, and Matt says he'd better go help Jackson. He says the meal is on him, and again Angie grieves for his financial largesse. She'll have to bring it up again, but not until they're through Christmas. She's played Scrooge often enough. Now it's time to be a loving angel of light.

chapter twenty

On Tuesday evening, Lillian Firestone dies in her chair, watching TV. There's been no hint of illness. She's just another old lady whose time had come. It falls to Angie to contact Jared with the news. Sherry suggests this, because of her association with him.

He takes the news well. It's possible he's even relieved. He says his mother was always such a complex, unhappy person, and that the peace she has now is well-earned. He says he'll come and go through her things. Personal items of family significance will be shared among his brother and Dorothy.

Angie says this all sounds very reasonable. What day would be good for him?

Jared hesitates. He's working on something new, and it's taking up a lot of his time. The weather's pretty bad, too. He's been stuck at home for several days—not that he minds. Winter's isolation can be very good for the creative process. He finds that interesting because so many painters, throughout time, tended to seek out the light and warmth. Not Bruegel, though. Much of Bruegel's work was an homage to the severe splendor of the Dutch winters. Does Angie know the painting, *Hunters in the Snow*? There's something almost primitive about how he handles the human form that reminds Jared of ancient cave paintings. The whole canvas is suffused with silvery aqua light as if he were inspired by looking into green agate.

"That sounds very interesting," Angie says.

"I'm boring you, I'm sorry."

"No, not at all."

"I guess I'm just getting used to the idea of her being gone."

"Grief is a process. If you like, I can send you some information about a group that meets at Lindell."

"Oh, no, I'm not much for that. I like to deal with things on my own."

"Of course."

Angie offers to start sorting Lillian's belongings for him, though the idea has no appeal. He says he can't ask her to do that and promises to come by next week, after the holiday.

"Unless I should come sooner. Do you need the room?" he asks.

"No, no not at all. We tend to lose residents this time of year. December and January."

"That's when people tend to die, you mean?"

"Yes."

"Well, winter can also be cruel. I suppose anything beautiful can have its darker side."

Angie says she's late for a meeting. He apologizes for taking up so much of her time. She asks him to be sure to stop by her office next week. Oh, what about a memorial service? Would it be convenient to hold it there, at Lindell? He says he'll confer with his brother and let her know.

The day is slow, her work all up to date. Foster calls and asks if she wants to help him choose a tree to put up at the professor's place. She agrees, though choosing a tree is fraught with difficult memories of her parents fighting about the expense. One year, Lavinia told Potter to take an axe and go out into a forest somewhere, then had to restrain him when he tried to because he was drunk. Angie and her brothers and sisters watched from the living room as their mother took the axe right out of his hand. Potter broke down crying. Lavinia put the axe in the basement, locked the door, and put the key somewhere he couldn't find it. That was the last time she challenged him to do something risky, something that might have had fateful consequences. The tree that year was one of the last off the lot, short, spindly, already dropping needles by the time they got it home. Angie wonders if her parents are working together to decorate whatever tree Lavinia's got over at her house and how it feels. Alma's presence would mitigate any bad memories, assuming there are any.

Foster's at the tree lot behind the Shop and Save when Angie arrives. He's got a dog with him, a black and white mutt. The dog is excited, and keeps circling Foster, wrapping his leash around his legs. Each time he does, Foster patiently redirects him.

"Who's this?" Angie asks.

"Barney. His parents are out of town, and he's boarding with us. I thought he could use an outing."

Barney sniffs Angie enthusiastically. She asks Foster if he remembers their childhood dog, Thaddeus. He does, especially how their mother disliked him.

"He threw up a lot. She was the one who dealt with it most of the time," Angie says.

"You cut your hair."

"Yeah."

They walk between two rows of trees, touching their branches, smelling their needles. Barney lifts his leg. Foster kicks fresh snow over the yellow puddle and moves on. He tells Barney to please not do that again, or to let him know beforehand that he has to go. Foster used to talk to Thaddeus; after Thaddeus, when their mother forbade them getting another dog, he had a slew of stuffed animals he named, cherished, and conversed with. Working in a vet's office suits him, though he finds it awful when the animals have to be put down. He's always felt closer to animals than to people. As far as Angie knows, he's never had a girlfriend, though there was one girl he saw for a while last year, Megan somebody.

Angie asks what happened to her. Foster looks at her skeptically. His photo-gray lenses give him a stylish air. The cold has put color in his cheeks. His blond hair falls charmingly in his eyes.

"Why?" he asks.

"Oh, I don't know. I just thought of her, all of a sudden."

"She got married."

"Really?"

"That's what I heard."

Angie wonders from whom. She realizes she doesn't know who his friends are. She feels bad about that.

She points out a nice spruce that's about five and a half feet tall. Foster regards it at length, though she can tell his mind's not on the tree. He chooses the next one over, finds the guy manning the lot, and pays in cash. They carry the tree to Foster's pick-up truck, which means Angie has to take Barney's leash. Barney's just as happy to be piloted by her until another dog comes into his line of sight and he completely freaks out. He strains, barks, wagging his tail furiously. He's a lot stronger than Angie thought he'd be, and she has to keep a tight grip.

Foster returns and takes the leash from her without a word. He says the dog's name firmly and Barney stands still. Angie says she's impressed. Foster explains that he's learned how to handle unruly dogs as part of his work. It's important to let them know that you're the leader of the pack.

With the tree onboard, Foster asks if she wants to go for coffee.

"What about Barney?" she asks.

"We'll bring him and let him lie under the table. He'll be a good boy."

They drive separately over to the mall, and a local shop Foster prefers to the chain coffee stores. The man behind the counter has blond dreadlocks. Everyone in there looks like a left-over hippie. They order and pick a table by the window. The heat is robust, and Angie removes her coat. Foster leaves his on. As he predicted, Barney lies under the table with his head on his paws.

Foster asks if she's looking forward to Christmas Eve.

"Oh, I think it will be fine. You know, the usual. Mom bossing everyone around."

"Except Dad will be there."

"Yeah, that's not usual."

"It's going to be a shit show."

"Why do you say that?"

Foster's smirk is quick and bitter. Angie can see he's afraid there will be some disagreement and tempers will flare. Or worse, that there will be dire moods, deep tension, and forced cheer. Angie says he needs to keep in mind that Alma—God bless her—has been a benign, steadying influence. She adds that he has to remember, too, that their mother is a much calmer person, sometimes even mellow. There's no reason to think things are going to blow up.

"What if Dad gets drunk?" Foster asks. The server deposits their coffee in large ceramic cups.

"We'll put him to bed. Won't be the first time."

Foster stirs away the fancy design the barista made with the steamed milk.

Angie says she really doesn't think there's anything to worry about, then senses his concern lies elsewhere.

"Are you wondering what will happen if they get back together?" she asks.

"I don't think that would be good for either of them."

"It's hard to say. They've known each other forever and still care for each other. They could do a lot worse."

It's that his understanding of their parents might shift that bothers him, though Angie doesn't state this. She knows people can occupy a static place in your mind, providing a constant, familiar backdrop, even if that backdrop isn't always pleasant or easy. Foster is used to Lavinia and Potter being at odds. That they might get along and be happy is a set change he doesn't know how to interpret. The uncertainty is hard for him to manage. He was always more sensitive to changes in routine than the rest of them. Angie suspects his insecurity has a lot to do with Lavinia saying more than once when he was young that she hadn't wanted another baby and yet there he was. His name, in fact, came from her arch remark that if she had any more children, they'd end up in foster care.

"How's work?" she asks.

"Good. The same. I'm wondering about applying to vet school."

"What, wait, really? That's awesome!"

The way he won't meet her eyes says he's been thinking about it for a while. He mentions that it was actually his boss's idea.

"Would you apply here, to Dunston U?" she asks.

"Somewhere out-of-state, probably."

"Really."

"I'm sick of this place."

"You'll change your mind come summer."

He laughs and says it's quite possible.

She says that she, too, is thinking of making a change, maybe resigning from Lindell, taking some time off.

Foster says working there must be boring. She says the residents keep her fresh, but she's not going to advance there unless or until her boss retires.

"What about doing what you were doing before?" Foster asks.

"Oh, I don't want to deal with people who can't get themselves out of bad situations."

"What about that one woman, what's-her-name, who wrote you that letter after she left her husband? She went back to school. Said it was all because of you."

Foster refers to Marcia Kingsley. Angie met with her several times at the women's shelter and urged her to get a divorce and move on with her life. The husband didn't seem like he was going to stalk her or attack her again (he'd struck Angie as pathetic, frustrated in his own life, and hugely remorseful about the assault on his wife). Marcia did all these things. Angie doesn't recall sharing the story with anyone. She's touched that Foster remembers.

"It's a stressful way to make a living," Angie says.

"No doubt, but you're very good at it."

Angie tells him that Matt's thinking of buying the bar and if he does, he wants her to work there with him.

"You, tend bar?" Foster asks. His tone causes Barney to lift his head.

"Or wait tables."

"Why would you want to do that?"

"Might be fun."

"Couples should never work together."

"Is that your considered opinion?"

"Well, look at what happened to Dad and Mary Beth."

Angie says they split up because Mary Beth, who never loved him in the first place, cheated on him. Even as she says this, she recalls Mary Beth crying in her bedroom when Potter was leaving. If she didn't love him, she certainly felt something close to it. What comes close to love that isn't love? Need?

227

Angie asks if Foster heard that she's been calling Potter up all the time.

"Yeah, Timothy told me."

Foster finishes his coffee. He has to get back to work. Angie asks if he wants her help decorating his tree. He says Sam and Timothy are coming by later, but she can come, too. She declines. She'll be up to ears in all of them the day after tomorrow.

She calls in and says she's taking the rest of the day off. She'll be in for a couple of hours tomorrow if anything urgent comes up.

When she gets home, she calls Matt. He says the bar is full of people in the holiday spirit. Does she want to come down? She says it doesn't sound like he's going to have a lot of time for her, and he agrees. He sounds tired, and she tells him to go home afterward and sleep hard.

She makes herself a sandwich. It occurs to her that her house doesn't have a single decoration, nothing to evoke the season. She brings up a box from the basement that has a couple of garlands. She secures one to the mantle with small nails she hammers very carefully, so as not to damage the wood too much. She lines the doorway to her bedroom the same way. It's not quite the effect she wanted, but at least the place seems more cheerful.

The box has photographs she's forgotten about, of her and her siblings taken long ago. Potter took all of them. Angie can't recall her mother ever holding a camera. Some scenes are composed, the kids lined up reluctantly on the couch, Angie in the middle so she could restrain unruly behavior from the others. The candid ones are surprisingly intimate: Angie helps Foster brush his teeth; Angie combs Marta's hair; Angie puts a Band-Aid on Timothy's forehead. She's not in every shot, but most of them, as if her father used her as a focal point to define what everyone else was doing.

There weren't any more photographs after Angie was about 13 or 14, which coincided with the time her parents split up. Her mother wasn't interested in capturing them as they got older. Maybe having them all underfoot every day was enough of a chronicle. Angie puts the photographs back in the box and returns it to the basement, where the furnace comes to life and hums.

When she gets back upstairs, she sees she's missed a call from Matt. He left no message. Maybe business at the bar tapered off, but Angie doubts that. After five straight days of snow, people are stir crazy and dying to get out.

She calls him back. The noise in the background confirms her thinking the place was packed. Matt says he's been on the phone with his mother, and Jen is now saying she doesn't want to go into rehab, that in fact, she doesn't really need it. She only agreed to it to get her mother to leave her alone.

"Back to square one," he says. There is no grief in his voice, only resignation. Angie takes this shift as progress.

"Looks like it."

"Listen, can you talk to her?"

"What, me?"

Matt chuckles. "Yes, you. You're a professional. You know your stuff."

"Yeah, but I don't know *her*."

"That's okay. I'd like to give her your number and tell her to call."

"What makes you think she will?"

"I'm just hoping."

"Okay."

Matt says he'll call Jen later tonight and urge her to reach out tomorrow. Angie says she'll have a light day at work, so it won't matter too much when she gets ahold of her. She'll keep her phone on her if she's away from her desk. Matt says she's the best. Angie is tempted to ask, "the best what?" and doesn't want to sound flippant. Then he has to go, the place is going nuts.

Angie's tired, all of a sudden. She decides to make it an early night.

chapter twenty-one

Angie oversees the dismantling of Lillian's room. The bed is stripped, items removed from the walls, boxed and labeled; personal items like her comb and hairbrush, also boxed and labeled. The closet is gone through, the quilted red box containing the stolen birth certificate handled with care. When everything is neatly arranged for Jared's inspection, Angie goes back to her office. She realizes she's looking forward to tomorrow night at her mother's. Even with every crazy thing she's endured in the last few weeks, the thought of sitting by the fire, enjoying the tree with her siblings, brings a wave of peace.

Matt's sister calls just before lunch. Just after she identifies herself the call drops. Angie doesn't know if she should try her back. She waits, then waits some more. After almost another fifteen minutes her phone rings again.

"Sorry about that," Jen says. Her voice is husky and deep. Angie has trouble matching this with the slight, agitated woman she saw through the window at Matt's apartment.

Angie waits for her to go on. The silence continues until Angie says, "Hello?"

"Yeah, I'm here. I was waiting for my mother to leave the room."

Angie asks how she's feeling. Jen says she's doing great. She just called because Matt was being such a butt about the whole thing. She wanted him to get off her back.

"He's worried about you," Angie says.

"Uh-huh."

"You sound skeptical."

"Skeptical is my middle name."

Jen says she knows Angie is supposed to tell her to go into rehab, but she's already decided she will, so there's no point in her listing out all the reasons why. Angie asked what persuaded her.

Another silence falls. Then Jen says she figures it beats being out in the cold trying to score another hit.

"For sure," Angie says. She tells her she's really glad she's going to get help. Jen clears her throat.

"So, you're Matt's girlfriend," she says.

"Yes."

"Is it serious?"

"Yes."

"Well, good luck with that."

Angie leans back in her chair.

"What do you mean?" she asks.

"Nothing."

Angie looks at the picture across the hall, of the water-smoothed rocks. She imagines the gentle rush and hiss, the sun warming her skin.

"He's got problems of his own, you know," Jen says.

"Everyone does."

"Drug problems."

"Past tense."

"You can believe that if you want."

Jen says he still uses, from time to time. If Angie hasn't found that out by now, she will soon enough. Angie thanks her for calling and tells her to have a lovely Christmas.

"Wait," Jen says. "My mother wants to talk to you."

"I'm late for a meeting."

"It'll only take a second."

The phone changes hands, and a lighter, easier voice comes on the line. The speaker introduces herself as Matt's mother and apologizes for taking up her time. She just wanted to thank Angie for talking to her daughter, and also for being so good to her son. She's heard so many nice things about her. She hopes they'll be able to meet in person someday soon.

Angie says she hopes so, too.

Matt's mother pauses.

"Is he all right?" she asks, after a moment.

"Matt? Yes, he's doing well."

"Thanks to you, I'm sure."

Angie says she hasn't done anything. Matt's mother says that's not true. Then she says she'll let her go and get back to work.

Angie packs up her stuff and leaves work for the weekend. She goes to the gym and uses the elliptical so hard her legs feel like rubber. At home, in the bathtub, with a glass of wine on the ledge, she reviews her brief conversations with Matt's sister and mother. She tells herself not to pursue anything. No confrontations. No scenes. Just a happy holiday mood.

After dinner, Matt calls. Angie lets him go to voice mail. He just wants to know how it went with his sister, and thanks her again for making time to talk to her. Later, she texts back, saying she's out doing last-minute shopping and that things are going to kick off at Lavinia's around three tomorrow afternoon. He can come to her place, and they can go over together if he wants.

After lunch the next day Angie swings by her mother's to drop off the guitar. She asks Alma to stash it in a closet. Alma looks at her haircut and nods. Then she puts the guitar in the laundry room and says it's a mighty generous gift. Her hard stare says she's wondering how things are going, clearly remembering their talk about Sharon, and Angie doesn't say a word.

233

Matt's waiting when she returns. He's helped himself to a cup of coffee. She's surprised he's early and doesn't say so. Nor does she say where she's been. She asks if he wants a quick bite before they head over, and he says he had a late breakfast. He hugs her hard, then kisses her. She kisses him back. He's shaved, and she misses the scratchy stubble just a little. He confesses to being nervous about seeing her whole family all at once. She reminds him that he's met everyone except the twins, and they're not that hard to deal with.

"You always say they are," Matt says.

"I guess I do. Well, Marta was fine when I saw her."

As they drive, Matt asks what he and Jen talked about. Angie says they talked about her going into rehab.

"Anything else?" he asks.

"No. Why?"

"She has a way of putting me down."

"She didn't do that."

Angie's glad he doesn't ask about the conversation with his mother and realizes he may not even know about it. If he brings it up, she'll say she forgot, that she was so busy trying to wrap up stuff at work it slipped her mind.

They're the first to arrive at Lavinia's. Alma greets Angie as if she hasn't seen her for days. Lavinia comes down the hall wearing a red velvet party dress and black crocodile high heels. She's cross. She tells everyone her shoes are too tight, and if nobody minds, she'd like to kick them off and run around in her bedroom slippers. Then she asks Angie why she cut her hair. Before Angie can answer, Lavinia takes her coat and Matt's and hands them to Alma, who drops them roughly on a chair by a fancy carved chest. They troop into the living room, where a ten-foot tree stands before the larger of two bay windows, opulently decorated in white and blue.

Matt looks around. "Nice," he says.

234

A minute later Potter comes in. He tells Angie her hair is great. He's wearing jeans and a button-down shirt. So's Matt, and they quickly seize on this and laugh. Angie's got on a wool dress she hasn't worn since the Christmas before. It's black and makes Matt's pendant stand out, though so far no one's commented on it.

Alma asks what everyone wants to drink, and Potter goes with her to help. Matt admires her efficiency and says he could use someone like her at The Watering Hole. Lavinia returns, the offending shoes removed and a pair of fluffy slippers in their place and sits down in an easy chair by the fire.

"What's this about The Watering Hole?" she asks.

Matt explains.

"You want to buy it, correct?" Lavinia asks.

Angie says to wait a second, how does she know about that? She says Timothy told her Matt was looking for financing.

"When?" Angie asks.

"Yesterday. No, the day before."

Angie looks at Matt. He says he mentioned it, that's all. Timothy said maybe his mother might be interested.

"Well, I'm not," Lavinia says. "But I know someone who is."

Alma returns with a tray of drinks and Potter distributes them around. Wine for Angie and Matt; champagne for Lavinia and Alma; club soda with a wedge of lime for Potter. He proposes a toast.

"Merry Christmas, one and all!" Five glasses are lifted, then sipped from. Potter sits in the empty chair on the other side of the fireplace. Alma returns to the kitchen where she says she's got a tray of cheese sticks that are about ready to come out.

Angie can feel the tension in Matt's body, even with a foot of space between them on the couch. The talk is of the recent snow, the cold, the taps Alma left dripping overnight, so the pipes won't freeze.

Matt said he did the same thing in his apartment. Angie says she didn't know you were supposed to do that.

"All these years living in the frozen north and you didn't know?" Potter asks. His voice is teasing, kind. Angie wonders if he's sneaking liquor somewhere. He's not usually so animated when he's sober.

When the conversation lulls, Lavinia tells Potter to share his scheme.

He puts his glass on the small table next to his chair and clears his throat. He doesn't speak for a moment. Then he says he and Mary Beth have come to a financial agreement. She's going to help him with a business venture. Her lawyer suggested it, rather than giving Potter a lump-sum settlement or alimony. Potter says the time has come for him to really be his own man, so when Lavinia mentioned that Matt here was looking for a partner, it sounded just great.

"He's not looking for a partner," Angie says. "Just financing."

"I'd be open to having a partner, as long as you'd help me run the place," Matt says.

Lavinia sips her champagne and gazes warmly at the tree, but Angie can see her listening to every word.

"I know what you're thinking," Potter says, looking right at Angie. "That having a man with a drinking problem work in a bar is like turning a diabetic loose in a candy store."

"Something like that."

"What better way to keep me on the straight and narrow?"

"It's true. If you can be around the thing that brings you down and stay afloat, then you know you're okay," Matt says.

"Maybe, but it sounds like wishful thinking to me," Angie says.

Potter says he's thought it all out. Matt will technically be his boss, and if he falls off the wagon, he'll get fired, or furloughed, or take a leave of absence, whatever.

"Matt needs a more reliable employee," Angie says, then regrets it when a tremor of hurt crosses Potter's face.

"I did great working for Mary Beth. Drinking never got in the way then, not until she . . . well, let's not get into all that," Potter says. Lavinia reaches over and pats his hand.

Timothy and Sam arrive. They have packages to put under the tree. Angie looks sternly at Timothy, who doesn't pick up on her meaning. Matt leans forward so he can speak more easily with Potter. They're friendly, affable with each other. Angie goes into the kitchen to see if Alma needs help. Alma's bastes a turkey in a pan, puts it back in the oven, then throws washed lettuce in a bowl. She says she's got everything under control, but Angie can keep her company if she wants.

Angie flops down on the banquette and tells her about Potter's plan to invest in The Watering Hole.

"Yeah, I heard," Alma says.

"Don't you think it's a stupid idea?"

"He's got to do something. He's starting to get underfoot, and I think your mom needs a break from him."

"Yeah, but . . ."

"Listen, honey, you worry about your dad too much. He's a big boy. Either he'll keep it together or he won't. I don't figure he can do much harm if he has one of his lapses. Why not let him try? It'll be good for him."

Angie is flooded with frustration. It passes, and her eyes remain dry. Alma sips from her glass of champagne and asks if she can get Angie anything. Angie asks if the cheese sticks are ready. They are. She takes the plate into the living room and offers it around. Timothy and Lavinia say they'll hold off for now. Potter ignores her because he's still talking to Matt, who also ignores her. Sam's by herself on the loveseat.

Angie joins her. Sam helps herself to a big handful of cheese sticks, then asks if Angie's okay.

"Yeah. It's just been a long, long year."

"Aren't they all?"

"For sure."

Angie lowers her voice and asks her if she knows anything about Timothy asking Lavinia about investing in the bar.

"He told me about it. I wasn't there when they talked," Sam says.

"When was this?"

"Two days ago? Matt came by. He had a CD of a new band he wanted Timothy to check out. I guess he's managing the bookings now."

"And he called Mom after that?"

"I guess." Sam sips her wine. "Why?"

"Nothing."

"You look like you smell something fishy."

"You know me. Always on the lookout for that rotten flounder."

Sam says she understands. If she's worried about her dad and Matt working together, she probably shouldn't be. They seem to get along pretty well. Angie agrees. She finishes her wine.

The light outside begins to drop, and the sky glows.

The twins burst into the room with their usual chaotic fanfare. Marta complains about how long it took to drive up, to which Maggie says it didn't take any longer than usual and that she kept offering to drive and Marta kept saying no. Maggie's wearing a floor-length dress patterned with vine and flowers. The dress looks vintage. Marta's in a dress, too, one that looks a lot like Lavinia's, only with a V-neck, not scoop neck. Angie gets up and gives each a brief hug. Maggie says her hair looks good. Then she tells Marta it doesn't look at all the way she said it did. Marta says she said Angie got bangs, and what are those, if not bangs? Angie introduces them to Matt. Matt stares at first one, then at the other.

"Whoa," he says.

"I know, that's what everybody says," Maggie says.

"When you said they were twins, I didn't know you meant *identical* twins."

They move on to Potter, then Lavinia, delivering a quick kiss to him, and a quick hug to her. Then Timothy gets swept up in their discussion of a new club they just went to in the city. He's polite, but Angie can tell he's not really interested. She joins Matt on the couch. He's still staring at her sisters, and for a bad moment, she wonders if he'll fall for one—or both of them. Then he turns to her and takes her hand.

Foster shows up a little later, saying there was an emergency at the vet's office. Lavinia says she hopes everything's all right.

"Dog got hit by a car, but it doesn't look too serious," Foster says.

Lavinia asks if he's still thinking about quitting. He says it depends on if he'll apply to vet school or not. Potter hasn't heard about that and asks some relevant questions about deadlines and costs. Foster says he'd apply for the fall after next and that his boss is willing to help with the tuition in exchange for giving him first dibs on offering him a position when he's got his degree.

"Wow, that sounds like a great deal!" Sam says. Foster approaches her and takes the seat Angie vacated. Alma announced that dinner is still a while off since the turkey seems to be larger than she thought.

"Maybe it grew," Matt says.

"Good one," Alma says.

Lavinia asks if they should open presents now, in that case. Everyone says they should wait. Angie offers to show Matt the rest of the house. He says sure, that sounds good. As they leave the room,

Marta calls out, "No fooling around, you two," and Angie flips her the bird.

They ascend the curving staircase, and Angie describes sliding down the banister after they first moved in. Poor Chip, she says. He had no idea how to deal with the sudden invasion of five children. His own boys, from his first marriage, were long grown then. In fact, of the sons, the only one who still talked to him (the other two were mad about things that had happened long ago) visited one summer from California and her mother fell for him. Angie supposes she thought she hid it well, but everyone knew, even Chip.

"Your mother had a thing for her husband's son?" Matt asked.

"You have to remember he was a lot older than she was. The son was much closer to her own age."

"Sounds wild."

"They didn't do anything. He turned her down."

They enter her old bedroom. The four-poster bed is still there, as is the flowery wallpaper. The mantle over the fireplace holds some of her mother's knick-knacks, mostly paperweights and small vases, currently empty. Angie says that in her day, it held a series of drawings she made during the phase when she thought she had some talent. Maggie quickly upstaged her with her own, far superior talent, and she stopped drawing.

Matt says it's hard, when siblings compete, even when they don't know that they are.

"What do you mean?"

"Well, Jen wanted to play the piano, and she took lessons that my mother struggled to pay for, but she wasn't much good. I was much better."

"So you inspired her to play."

"I guess."

240

"What else did she like to do?"

"Chase boys. Until they started chasing her. Then she didn't have to work so hard at it."

Angie asks if she's pretty. Matt says she is, though not as pretty as Angie.

"Yeah? Well, I'm not as pretty as my sisters," she says.

"Bull! Besides, they look totally high maintenance."

"They are. They're spoiled as hell. My mother gives them money to live on."

Angie can see Matt wondering what that must be like.

"Look, about my mentioning the bar to Timothy, I hope you don't mind," he says.

"I thought you were going to let me approach my mother."

"I could tell you didn't want to."

That's true. She didn't.

"So you decided to find another way," she says.

"I just told Timothy I was looking for financing. He was the one who suggested your mother. I said I felt uneasy talking to her myself, so he offered to."

"Did you *know* he would offer when you started telling him about it?"

"No."

"Are you *sure?*"

"Hey, what is this?"

Angie says it's nothing, she's just a little uptight. Her family always makes her that way. And she's never been too fond of this time of year. Matt says he knows what she means.

They stand at the window together, looking out into the deep snow-covered yard. There are spotlights turned on a row of poplar trees. Angie describes hiding there when she was younger and needed time to herself. Matt says in a house this big, it seems weird she couldn't just have come in here and locked her door.

"My mother had a thing against locked doors," she said.

"Probably prudent, if you're a parent."

It was his sister's unlocked door that led his mother to first discover her drug habit. Angie says nothing. Matt seems to sense her isolation, so he asks her about what she was like as a teenager. She says she was lonely and pissed-off.

"What did you want most in those days?" he asks.

Angie reflects. That time was so hard, so full of longing, like a constant ache.

"I guess I wanted someone like you," she says.

They embrace, kiss, stop kissing, and pull apart, but still hold hands.

"That's a really sweet thing to say," he says.

"And I'm not a sweet person."

"Get out."

She asks if he's serious about working with her dad at The Watering Hole. He says yeah, sure, of course. She cautions him. He's known to be flaky when it comes to keeping any kind of schedule.

Matt says it doesn't really matter. Potter can do as much, or as little, of the day-to-day stuff as he wants.

Angie asks Matt what he'll ask Potter to put in, investment-wise. Matt says about two thirds if he can.

"That's a boatload."

"It is. It depends on what his wife or soon-to-be-ex-wife is willing to spring for on his behalf, but it's worth asking."

"And you'll borrow the rest?"

"I'm sure going to try."

Angie says she hopes the bar doesn't fail, or everyone's going to lose a lot of dough. Matt says it's a college town, it's almost impossible for a bar to fail. It will do fine and make money for them both.

Alma calls up the stairs that dinner's almost ready and that she misread the damn meat thermometer before.

They gather in the dining room. Potter sits at the head, with Lavinia at the other end. Angie thinks how wonderful things would have been if they'd stayed together, he'd had the kind of money Chip did, and that this had been their house all along.

Idle fantasies.

I can dream, can't I?

The meal is surprisingly pleasant. Angie doesn't talk much but enjoys whatever the others have to say. Alma reminisces about growing up in the country outside of Dunston, and the hand-made gifts her family exchanged. She says they could have afforded store-bought presents because her dad was a plumber and did pretty well. He was just cheap. Marta and Maggie ask if anyone remembers the time they got matching bunny outfits and wore them for days until Lavinia ordered them to change. Foster says Angie was the one who issued the order, but maybe it was at Lavinia's request. Sam shares details of her only Christmas away from Dunston when she lived for a brief time in LA. Her upstairs neighbor was a little Japanese woman who turned out to be a prostitute. Her name was Suki, and Christmas was a day off for her, so she came down to Sam's apartment and made her miso soup. Sam pauses and then says she wonders whatever happened to her, and where she is right now.

Matt keeps trying to catch Angie's eye from across the table. Angie realizes she's been avoiding looking at him. She smiles, and he visibly relaxes. She reviews her odd phone conversation with his sister. Trash talking on Jen's part, or truth? How would she know if he's using drugs since she's not around? That point of logic failed to occur to her yesterday, and Angie knows she jumped—or was tempted to jump— to bad conclusions. If love is giving someone a chance, among all the things it is or can be, suspicion and disbelief must be suspended—at least long enough for the heart to open.

Later, after the gifts are shared, and Matt plays a lovely tune on his new guitar—the first sight of which left him briefly at a loss for words—Angie again finds herself at a window, gazing into the dark. Reflected in the glass are all the people in the room behind her, some of whom stand and wander to another corner of it, leave to use the bathroom and return, or sit comfortably, like her parents, side by side before the fire. Matt's on the couch, his head cocked to better hear his notes, his face a study in concentration. In this softened image, his soul seems both visible and true, free of any harsh experience. Perhaps the image is real, a lie, or merely a cause for hope. Angie doesn't know. What is sure is that the days will lengthen bit by bit and that it's lovely to stand here now, eager for that rising light, and the kinder season ahead.

THE END

about the author

Anne Leigh Parrish is the author of *What Nell Dreams; Maggie's Ruse; The Amendment; Women Within; By the Wayside; What Is Found, What Is Lost; Our Love Could Light The World;* and *All The Roads That Lead From Home.*

about the press

Unsolicited Press was founded in 2012 and is based in Portland, Oregon. The small press publishes fiction, poetry, and creative nonfiction written by award-winning authors.

Learn more at www.unsolicitedpress.com

CPSIA information can be obtained
at www.ICGtesting.com
Printed in the USA
BVHW070621230321
603190BV00003B/145